About the Author

The author has a Bachelor of Criminology, majoring in Criminal Justice, from Griffith University in Brisbane. She has worked as a parole probation officer for over twelve years in Queensland and South Australia. She is currently retired and living at Bungawalbin, New South Wales, with her partner.

The Man With The Cold Steel Blue Eyes

Chris Reynolds

The Man With The Cold Steel Blue Eyes

Olympia Publishers
London

www.olympiapublishers.com
OLYMPIA PAPERBACK EDITION

A CIP catalogue record for this title is
available from the British Library.

ISBN: 978-1-80074-916-0

First Published in 2023

Olympia Publishers
Tallis House
2 Tallis Street
London
EC4Y 0AB

Printed in Great Britain

Dedication

I dedicate this book to all the lonely and isolated people out there that have lost contact with their family and friends.

Acknowledgements

I would like to thank my family and friends who not only encouraged me to complete this book but also contributed financially to the publication. I'll be forever thankful and grateful for your assistance, you all know who you are.

Chapter One

Carol and Rosslyn were excited about being invited to sing at the Redcliffe Bowling Club on Saturday night. It would be Rosslyn's first paid performance after she had made the finals in a singing contest for older contestants in Brisbane. They had booked a hotel room for the night as they knew they would be having a few drinks and would be home late. They left Russell Island on the boat at five in the afternoon.

"It looks like Shelley's off to work again," said Carol.

They'd noticed her on numerous occasions walking down main roads dressed in skimpy clothing with the essential high heels on her way to work, and while they did not feel sorry for her, they both thought, *poor bitch.*

"She's had a hard life," noted Carol.

Carol knew her antecedents as she had been a parole officer before she retired.

After they booked into the hotel at Redcliffe, they went to the bowling club to meet Patricia, who was also a finalist in the competition. The gig was a huge success and they arrived back at their room at midnight. They threw themselves into bed, totally knackered, and tried to sleep.

"I can't sleep. I'm so excited," said Rosslyn.

Rosslyn was running on adrenaline from performing in public, thrilled about how the audience appeared to enjoy themselves. Carol who liked watching old movies turned on the television to find that all that was on, was infomercials.

"What's this rubbish, don't they have any late-night movies on any more?" exclaimed Carol.

"Not since we were girls," laughed Rosslyn.

"What's that noise?" they both said in unison.

All night, they could hear comings and goings.

"I think we've booked into a hotel that rents rooms by the hour. You know, things that go bump in the night," said Carol, as it reminded her of the time her long deceased mother booked into the Biltmore Hotel in Kings Cross in Sydney. "One of the old aunts that lived in Randwick had recommended the hotel as a suitable place to stay. I remember Mum being hypervigilant all night, reminding us to lock the door and claiming it might have been all right during the war years but was a definite house of ill repute by the nineteen seventies."

"I think you're right," said Rosslyn.

"Are you tired?"

"Well, no," said Rosslyn.

"Me neither, let's get out of here."

They left the hotel at three a.m. to drive home, and as they approached Deception Bay, a heavy fog descended, along with night road works, made driving difficult. Rosslyn was a good co-pilot and encouraged Carol to continue driving through Sheldon toward Capalaba, an area they knew well but could hardly recognise due to the fog. The creepy environs had them on edge.

It was October the thirty-first and as they approached Capalaba, Rosslyn commented, "It looks like someone's hung a mannequin out of the window of that vacant house."

What looked like a lifeless doll was a body hanging from the upper level of an old Queenslander. It was hanging from the security bars and they would have had to climb the steps and somehow thrown themselves over the verandah whilst tying a rope around their neck, which looked impossible to do. They recognised the flimsy red dress and the matching shoes from yesterday similar to what Shelley had been wearing.

They both had a good look before Carol exclaimed, "Oh my God, it looks like Shelley"

Carol insisted that she was right and turned the car around for a closer look. As they were checking out the scene, they were approached by an older lady who was ashen and in shock.

"I've called the police."

They looked at the doll-like figure that hung from the window, noticing the shoes neatly lined up on the steps. As they observed the scene, they both agreed that it was Shelley.

"Do you believe me now? She's wearing the same outfit she had on yesterday afternoon when we saw her on the jetty as we left to go to Redcliffe."

Even though they had no sleep, they were not tired when they got home, they were in shock.

"It's not every day you see a dead body."

Carol had only ever seen one dead body before and could not get over the fact that the dead looked like lifeless dolls. For the next few weeks, they checked news reports and Carol asked people she knew about the police investigation. It appeared her death was deemed a suicide.

Chapter Two

Stranger chose his victims carefully. He'd only been convicted of one violent sex crime and sentenced to twenty-five years' in prison. He was now a registered sex offender. With an IQ of one hundred and fifty, he was an above average manipulator and intelligent enough to comply with all his parole conditions, which were numerous. He never had a parole violation during his fifteen years of supervision. He was tested for drug and alcohol use at home and at his appointments, where he had to discuss his living situation, relationships, and sexual fantasies with his parole officer.

He remembered Carol Plummer was his allocated Parole Officer before she retired. She'd been firm but fair and ensured he complied with his conditions but knew he never went along with the spirit of his order and knew his compliance was superficial.

He only made one mistake in that he murdered a woman that he was in a relationship with. She was underage and he was now a registered sex offender and paedophile and would be under the scrutiny of authorities for many years. He knew he had murdered at least ten other women and it was rumoured within the police and parole service that he was a serial killer that had never been caught for his crimes. His main area of expertise was sexual games that included ligature strangling whilst having sex with his victims.

He attended the gym daily, working on weights and core

strength –a habit he had picked up in prison. He continued his fitness regime after his release, and maintained his fitness as he works as landscape gardener.

I must admit, I am proud of my lean, fit body. It's easier to pick up women if you don't look like a scumbag, I now have to report any changes of circumstances to the police.

"They know my car registration, address, and employment details and can check on me at any time," he muttered to himself.

I've always chosen my victims carefully. My last victim was a woman who worked as a prostitute on a casual basis. Her family had disowned her years ago and her children were living with her ex-husband and were too embarrassed to be seen in her company. She was no stranger to unorthodox sexual behaviour and willingly participated in my games. After she died, I hung her from a window of an abandoned house, neatly placing her high heel shoes on the steps. That was the final insult, boy she loved those shoes.

Police and forensic investigators deemed the death as suicide. I couldn't believe my good luck or their stupidity. I'd got away with murder.

Chapter Three

Carol completed a road trip she and Rosslyn had planned to go on when they retired. They travelled the length and breadth of the country for a few years and felt revitalised and were in a positive head space for their future.

Just thinking about some of the people she'd supervised over the years made Carol laugh. All of them flawed, and that's only the staff members. Seriously, some of the clients or offenders knew no boundaries to their behaviour. The working girls were some of her favourites as far as being characters. Some of the psychopaths or sociopaths were entertaining with their lies and deceptions. Some of them were downright scary.

t Carol could look a little stern and serious, but underneath it all she was a very colourful character with an extraordinary vocabulary for profanity. She was always well presented, had the kindest blue eyes, and was particularly good at obtaining information from her clients. They tended to trust her and tell her everything. Thus, with their permission, she became the queen of INTEL (intelligence) as far as supplying reliable information to police, specifically in relation to drug manufacturing and sometimes murder.

Carol was at a loose end and attended the Magistrates Court at Cleveland for some light entertainment. The waiting room was full of well-dressed, first-time offenders who had figured out or were advised that if they dressed neat and tidy, it would show respect to the court and could lessen their sentence or penalty.

These offenders were usually supported by their worried families. The recidivist would not bother dressing up and arrived in their usual attire of T-Shirts, jeans or track pants.

The public is always welcome, and proceedings commence at nine a.m. Carol was sitting in the public gallery and looked over and saw Denise Hargreaves, retired Police Prosecutor, and gave her a wave. Carol always thought that attending the Magistrates Court on a Monday was quite a good snapshot on what's going on in any community.

Some of the offenders Carol saw were new to the system and others she observed knew the ropes and are what they call recidivists. Driving, drugs, and anti-social behaviours are all represented. People going for the 'trifecta', assault, obstruct, and resist police, when under the influence or under arrest are fools. Because if they knew what she knew, it's easier in the long run to go quietly. All domestic violence order applications are heard in a closed court, in that the public are asked to leave the court for a while during those proceedings.

As the court officer called out names, the next in line were a couple of known offenders Carol had supervised over the years. Dennis 'fat boy' Hunt, charged with disqualified driving again! Amazing, she thought, as he was a well-known drug dealer and junkie on the methadone program and had never been convicted of a drug offence. It made Carol wonder as she thought to herself, *he's either an informant, lucky, or protected by corrupt police.*

Chapter Four

Her friend, Denise Hargreaves, had been a police prosecutor and most criminals were scared of her. She was the most organised person Carol had ever seen during her working life. When Denise decided to retire, she had no real plans other than to take it easy, and go on a few short cruises to the islands and to look after her large garden. She'd seen it all during her time. Recidivist offenders that never seem to realise some crimes never pay. She deemed her life and career as a success and was looking forward to retirement. Policing is not rocket science. Generally, police know all disqualified drivers and their addresses and the traffic branch targets the recidivists. In addition, they know who does criminal activity in their area and work hard to harass them enough to relocate. She had also seen her share of stupid behaviour committed by those under the influence of alcohol or drugs.

To those who were misguided souls, she appeared to be a mother figure. To those who were hardened criminals, she was a she-wolf. She supported rehabilitation and assistance to those who were suitable, she knew that most of them breached their community-based orders by noncompliance to the condition by committing further offences. Seventy percent breached probation and community service orders. Seventy percent of police work related to domestic violence, which in her mind was a sad reflection on society. How attitudes had changed during her time in policing towards the issue of domestic violence.

She was a friend of Carol Plummer's, who was her favourite parole officer as she had a great sense of humour and a great sense of justice that focussed on community safety.

Some of Carol's friends and former colleagues were in attendance. Kathryn Harrison, a legal aid solicitor, is acting as a friend of the court today. Margo Greaves was there on behalf of the Probation and Parole Service.

The next well- known offender before the court was charged with obtaining and maintaining a relationship with a person under the age of sixteen. Carol remembered Stranger well. He looked smaller than she remembered. He was a fit looking forty-five-year-old who spoke softly and was dressed neat and tidy. His matter was adjourned for a month to allow him to apply for legal aid. He did not look happy.

Chapter Five

They met for lunch and ordered a substantial healthy meal as they all needed a boost after the morning's activities. It was good to catch up. Denise and Carol discussed their retirement activities and had a good laugh about being such creatures of pathetic behaviour in attending court on a Monday. Kathryn and Margo were amused by their travel stories and added that they were still working their butts off.

During lunch, the discussion turned to the two recidivists. The one charged with the alleged child sex offence was well known to them all.

Kathryn said, "Stranger has been charged with maintaining a sexual relationship with a child he had met over the internet."

"Some things never change, do they?" offered Carol.

"The child's mother has made these allegations after she found and read her daughter's Facebook entries and of course he is denying it," added Kathryn.

The allegations and possible consequences were discussed between those gathered for lunch. Carol remembered him well.

"He was the coldest, most calculating coward I have ever met, very bright and manipulative."

She could still remember their first meeting over fifteen years ago. Her impression had not changed during this time.

"He's a diagnosed psychopath, you know. His psychologist told me in a moment of weakness. You know how psychologists can be, don't you, Margot?"

They both knew it was hard to get any information or feedback as working for Corrective Services to them was a conflict of interest.

"The one who disclosed the diagnosis only told me because I had referred him back for further treatment. Her exact words were that he had no conscience or empathy for others and was totally self-centred."

"Then she told you to fuck off with your referral?" added Denise, which made everyone at the table laugh, firstly because it was half true and secondly, they knew what a hopeless case Stranger had been.

"How many psychologists does it take to change a light bulb?" said Denise with a smirk on her face.

In unison they replied, "One to a hundred, it depends on whether the light bulb wants to change."

Hardy ha ha, thought Carol. She always called him the man with the cold, steel-blue eyes. Just thinking about him gave her the creeps and a feeling that bad things were going to happen.

After Margo and Kathryn finished their lunch and returned to court, Denise and Carol had another coffee and discussed their retirement. They both agreed that they were getting bored with the good life and missed the stress and excitement of their previous jobs. They decided to set up a Private Investigator office. They'd call the firm 'Hargreaves and Plummer Investigations' and thought that, with their accumulated skills, they could offer a service to clients that were discreet, organised, professional and agreed they could utilise their contacts.

They agreed to meet next week to sort out their premises, advertising, and the cost of setting up their new enterprise and what they would charge for their services.

Chapter Six

"Fuck! Fuck! Fuck! I can't believe the bitch's mother has made a complaint and the matter is going to court." Stranger was furious as these allegations were going to be a problem for him as a registered sex offender. "I could go back to prison for a long time."

He still couldn't believe he was convicted over twenty years ago when he had a sexual relationship with the only woman he had ever loved.

"It was a shame she was under the age of sixteen," he said as he reminisced about the past.

On a positive note, he had a child with another woman who left him after he was convicted of murder and child sex offences. His daughter would be in her twenties as far as he could remember. He was very proud of her and by all reports she was good looking, successful, and lived in Los Angeles. He had never met her.

He remembered how he had boasted to his old parole officer about his daughter and told her that he would like to get in touch with her. He had even shown her a photo of his daughter, whom he thought was good looking and much like him in regards to her intelligence and sharpness of features. He remembered his parole officer had told him that he would not be able to travel overseas while on parole but may be able to in the future. It would depend on the Police Service giving him permission as an Australian National Child Offence Register (ANCOR) offender. This would depend on no further charges and/or convictions.

He thought deeply about the impact of the new allegation and devised a plan to have the allegations withdrawn or disappear.

Chapter Seven

Denise and Carol found suitable premises close to the courthouse and had obtained their private investigators licence and opened for business.

"Hargreaves and Plummer, Private Investigators, your problem is our resolve," Carol was laughing as she put the key in the door.

They figured they would have to charge five hundred dollars a day plus expenses if they ever got any clients that were willing to pay.

"Thank God for our superannuation," chimed in Denise.

They were not overrun with clients but they found a steady flow of work from the retail sector regarding checking security tapes looking for staff thieving from their employers. They found this work as about as exciting as watching water boil so enlisted Rosslyn, who had worked in the retail industry and was terrific at observing sleight of hand movements at the till and other activities of thieves.

She'd claimed, "It's like watching the hands of card dealers at the casino."

They began to build a reputation for finding missing persons. They were specifically good at finding young pubescent girls and boys who ran away from their families to pursue an exciting life. Many drifted to and hung around with known criminals that pursued the same lifestyle. Hargreaves and Plummer knew where to look and who to contact within the police and probation service. Both services usually had fairly reliable information as to last known and previous residences of the person of interest.

Although they found surveillance work tedious and the hours long, they persisted sometimes into the early hours of the morning. The late nights nearly killed them as, since their retirement, they were used to going to bed at nine-thirty p.m. They'd had a good laugh about that, sitting in pubs and clubs to the early hours, eavesdropping.

'Cheers big ears' became their catch cry as they overheard conversations about some of the people they were looking for as all criminals love to talk and gossip. They had been very successful in locating the misled young people who thought they were doing something exciting. Not all returned home, but at least their parents or those that cared knew they were alive and well. They did a lot of surveillance work at night, and knew they would have to have better cover during daylight hours and considered getting a dog. No one would think twice about a couple of older women walking around the neighbourhood with a dog.

After a late night looking for lost children, Carol and Denise arrived at their office at about eleven-thirty a.m. They'd had a big night 'big earsing' and located the missing girl they were looking for at three a.m. They did their usual routine, and encouraged the girl to contact home. When they arrived at the office, Rosslyn, had identified another thief at the register. They were impressed as the tapes had been inspected by the retailer's security people. What a marvellous asset Rosslyn was as she took phone calls, opened the office on time, and diligently passed on all messages without pay. She was Carol's partner in life and loved being involved with the firm.

By the time Carol and Denise arrived at work, they reckoned

that it was time for lunch. As they were about to leave, two clients arrived.

"Christ, where do these girls get their fashion sense?" muttered Rosslyn.

They always made Carol laugh, probably her 'besties' as far as working girls go. She'd always wondered where they got their outfits. Down to the ground leopard-skin coat, fuck me boots with extremely high heels, mini skirt, and top. The other one wore tight jeans and lots of leather. They dressed as black widows, not quite diesel dykes, but it had the same effect. That 'fuck off, don't bother me look', a couple of tattoos added to the effect. Carol was lightly dressed, jumper and coat. Christ it was cold outside.

They both appeared agitated and said in unison, "We have a problem that we want investigated."

Denise and Carol looked at each other and sighed.

It was decided that they would eat lunch in the office and Carol sent her real 'bestie', Rosslyn, out for sandwiches and drinks. To her surprise, the girls did not order alcohol. *Good for them,* she thought. It must be a serious problem as these two had been around the block a few times and liked a drink.

They both looked worried! Janet had always been the verbose one of the pair, while Marcia was quiet and thoughtful.

Janet told them, "A good friend of ours, Shelley, was murdered. It was deemed a suicide, which is bullshit."

She added that she and Marcia had pursued all avenues, and no one was interested as the matter had been finalised. They both knew the victim.

Carol looked at Denise and whispered, "I'll tell you later."

What a sad and lonely life. The victim, Shelley, was in her forties, a street kid when she was younger, and an accessory after the fact to a murder where she was relocated to another city under the witness protection system. She came up well to the trifecta as far as addictions went, alcohol, heroin, and sex. She was always very needy and wanting to please.

Marcia and Janet claimed, "Shelley would never have hung herself as she could barely tie her own shoelaces let alone a noose."

They named their main suspect. Denise and Carol nearly fell off their chairs. Their eyes lit up, and Carol could personally feel the adrenaline starting to kick in and looked at Denise, who was trying to contain a smile. Then they told them why he was the main suspect. They agreed to take the case and would report any progress to the girls weekly,,. Boy, they'd always been a good source of INTEL for Carol over the years. The girls agreed to pay their bill on a weekly basis and would pass on anything they heard.

Denise and Carol could hardly contain themselves after the girls left. Come hell or high water, they'll get that bastard, Stranger, one day.

Chapter Eight

Peter Stranger knew he had to do something about the allegations against him. He was not allowed any contact with his victim, the underage, pubescent girl, and realised he would have to intimidate and/or frighten the girl's mother so she would drop the charges. His plan may not be that simple, as the Police Service may charge him with the alleged offences; he was not sure where he stood. But he did know how to intimidate from a distance. The odd phone call where no one spoke and breathed heavily into the phone, and hang up. His preferred method was to rattle around backyards, making noise and not being seen. That really puts the wind up and scares the shit out of people as he had done it before with great effect.

His life, however, had become predictable since he was released on parole. He was offered employment with a local landscaper who knew him before he went to prison. His employer a friend who had given him a place to live, a nice two-bedroom house on five acres which was located in one of the nicer suburbs in Brisbane. He rarely went out at night due to the physical nature of his work and he realised he was getting old and tired. On the other hand, he knew he would have to make a move towards solving his legal problem. He had made a few phantom phone calls as he called the mother's number when he was at work, travelling between jobs. No problem there, as he made the calls from phone boxes along the way. Untraceable really, no fingerprints left, and he was starting to get a kick out of making the calls. The girl's mother started to sound apprehensive, like she was starting to get scared.

His fantasies began again, and he knew he should see his psychologist but then again, in his mind, there was no such thing as should. Hell, he thought, he was starting to enjoy life again, thinking his thoughts, visualising his activities, and the phantom calls were getting him excited and aroused.

He had to get back into the saddle, so to speak, as he felt he was getting a bit middle-aged and boring. Nothing excited him more than the chase. His first thoughts went to how to intimidate his witness enough to drop the charges. His second thought that was becoming a fantasy was to choose another victim for his sexual pursuits.

A plan started to form. He'd have to get home from work, rest up or have a nap, then hit the streets again in the early hours of the morning. *Hell,* he thought *I could just get up a few hours earlier and do my good deeds and cruising before I go to work at five a.m. Rattle a few cages between three a.m. to five a.m. for a while, and then on other nights go cruising down Fortitude Valley to look for my next victim. I could dress up in camouflage to do my disturbances, knock over a few wheelie bins, and remove or misplace items in the mother's backyard. Then afterwards I could put on my high visibility clothes and go to work.*

His lips twitched with the anticipation of what he was going to do. He decided then and there that he would need to change his tactics when he trolled for another victim. He would need to dress neat and tidy to enable himself to chat up the 'girls' that worked as street hookers in Fortitude Valley, where he would have to use his charm and influence. He knew they all liked to party and used alcohol and drugs, which would be a great enticer to his schemes. He also knew a lot of them worked as strippers and lap dancers at a local hotel in Brisbane where he intended to visit and check out the local scene for opportunities.

Chapter Nine

Denise and Carol commenced their surveillance on their person of interest, Stranger. They initially borrowed a police dog that had failed to pass its training. He was a large German Shepherd that was affectionate, well behaved, who came when he was called, and was sociable with other dogs. The only problem with him was that when he was called to attack, he would not know when to stop. He failed his test to be a police dog after he ripped up several dummies. Therefore, he was deemed as unsuitable for police work. Carol bought him and named him Richmond. He was taken home and became part of the family, living with Carol and her partner, Rosslyn Flynn.

Denise and Carol walked Richmond to a local park close to where Stranger lived at Sheldon. They'd been on surveillance duties for a few weeks now, walking the dog around the neighbourhood and looking inconspicuous, as all old-aged pensioners tend to do.

As Carol's mother used to say, 'You reach a certain age and you become invisible'. Carol didn't believe her at the time, but since retiring, she now knew it to be true. No one takes any notice of a couple of old girls walking a dog.

Stranger's routine during the last two weeks did not appear to change. They followed him in Carol's campervan, which they had parked opposite his house. He appeared to go straight to work and pick up his employer's company truck to travel to his next job site. His duties varied. He worked hard, tree lopping and removal, mowing lawns, trimming hedges, and building retaining walls. He stopped for lunch and made phone calls from phone boxes between job sites. Nothing exciting appeared to happen during his work hours.

They decided they would have to watch him overnight. The campervan was set up well and had been parked in the street opposite Stranger's for the last few weeks, so it would not look out of place. It was decided that one would watch when the other one slept in the comfortable bed. A perfect set up for surveillance, coffee could be had, and the windows were tinted so it was hard to see inside. They found it hard to get close to the house as it was situated in an area that were between five and ten acres. His house and yard were well maintained, neat and tidy, like the man himself.

Carol and Denise saw movement in his yard the following week at about three a.m. Their persistence appeared to be paying off. Richmond had started to growl, which in turn made them all alert and ready for action. He was on the move. They followed at a distance as there was no traffic on the road at this time of night. He appeared to be heading for the local shopping centre at Capalaba.

Stranger zipped around a few corners and headed towards the industrial area behind the shops. Denise and Carol had to hang back as it would have been too obvious that they were following him. They stayed behind, kept out of sight, and parked behind the shopping centre that backed onto a block of units. They saw his headlights coming their way and ducked for cover under the dashboard. They did not think he saw them but started to become paranoid about using the camper for surveillance. Stranger stopped down the road and jumped the back fence to the units. They wondered what he was doing as they could not see him and could not get out of the van without being observed.

"What is he doing?" asked Carol.

All they could hear was a lot of banging around, he certainly was not creeping around casing the joint. He came back to his car and headed off again. They decided not to follow, went home, as they needed to change their modus operandi. They thought they'd call Jed Atkins to assist in the night operations that they decided to continue as they were mystified by what he was doing behind the units at Capalaba.

Jed was an ex-army Special Air Forces officer that worked in security. He had given them their first job checking security tapes. Denise called him and explained their situation. He agreed to help.

Chapter Ten

They met Kathryn Harrison and Margo Greaves outside the Cleveland Magistrates Court on Stranger's next court appearance and agreed to meet for lunch at the Coffee Club.

The Depositions Clerk called Peter Stranger to court and mispronounced his name, as in stranger not stranga. Carol and Denise tried not to laugh at him as he appeared pissed off at the mispronouncing of his name.

Stranger appeared agitated and was represented by Kathryn, who advised the court that legal aid had not been approved and adjourned the matter for another month.

Janet and Marcia were in the public gallery watching proceedings. Then their names were called out.

"Oh dear, what have these two been up to?" Carol muttered to herself as the charges were read out in court.

They had both been charged with soliciting and drug offences. Carol knew that, with their reputations, they could not stay out of trouble for long. They both knew the procedure and had their matters adjourned for a legal aid application.

Carol and Denise saw them in the foyer after the adjournments and Denise told them, "Come and see us in our office tomorrow for a chat."

They actually looked embarrassed and agreed to do what was asked, they did not look pleased with themselves.

Denise and Carol met Kathryn and Margo for lunch and told them what they had been up to with their new business venture.

Denise told them, "We have been following Stranger for the last month, he appears to make his phone calls from phone boxes and has been acting suspiciously at the back of the Capalaba Shops."

Both Kathryn and Margo looked at each other, deciding whether they would tell them what was in the police briefs.

Denise told them, "I'm going to try to obtain a copy from the Police Prosecutor I trained."

She knew it would be unethical for them to disclose the contents of the brief, but also knew how to bluff for the result she wanted. Kathryn looked like she was in deep thought and nodded occasionally during their description of the surveillance they had conducted.

They told Kathryn, "We have hired Jed Atkins to do the surveillance work and follow him at night for the next few months as we need to find out what he does after hours."

Kathryn then told them, "The Police have not supplied the brief on Stranger to date as they were having trouble with their witness."

So, in reality, she could not supply the brief even if she was inclined to do so.

She advised, "The witness or the complainant resides in units behind the Capalaba shops and has suddenly got 'cold feet' in that she was not sure whether to pursue the charges against Stranger."

"The police, on the other hand, were not sure they had enough evidence to prosecute without their witness and feared the matter would be Neto'd (not enough evidence to offer)."

"Now his expedition to Capalaba makes sense," declared Denise. "The bastard is intimidating the witness."

"We'll have to increase our surveillance and get some hard

evidence."

Kathryn and Margo had seen the police brief on the 'girls' and didn't mind discussing this at all.

Margo said, "If you can believe it, they had allegedly solicited and offered drugs to a police officer in an unmarked police car in Fortitude Valley."

Carol thought that sounded like them, "I believe it, as Janet once hailed a police car thinking it was a taxi as she is illiterate and can't read or write to save her life."

They all agreed to stay in touch and told Kathryn and Margo that they would let them know of any further developments from Jed Atkins' surveillance.

Chapter Eleven

Rosslyn opened the office at eight-thirty a.m. and went through the messages and collected the mail.

Jed arrived as Carol and Denise pulled into their respective car spaces. Jed was built like a brick shithouse, not unlike an ex-crim, neatly dressed, bulked up arms and body due to his addiction to fitness and health. He was a gregarious character who loved to talk about his talents and exploits when he was in the army and when he was working in security. He had a quizzical look on his face, almost mischievous.

He gave Hargreaves and Plummer details on how he was going to conduct surveillance on Stranger. By his description, he was going to do the full SAS routine, camouflage clothes, night vision glasses, and a non-descript pursuit vehicle, his wife's Hyundai Excel.

They both told him that they'd followed Stanger during work hours and that they wanted him watched between ten p.m. to three a.m. if he could manage that for them. He reckoned he could do it and would be able to extend his hours if needed.

When they outlined their commitments and Stranger's antecedents, he said, "I'll give you mates' rates."

Janet and Marcia arrived at noon, dressed rather conservatively in jeans, shirts, and runners. They were designer clothes, probably knocked off or stolen from the local shops.

Marcia told them, "We have been doing a bit of investigating ourselves."

They looked sheepishly around the room, then claimed, "We have spoken to all our contacts and have been told that Stranger has been to Fortitude Valley chatting up chicks and offering drugs for sex."

Then they added, "The gossip that is spreading amongst the working girls is about who is missing, possibly murdered, after another Brisbane prostitute was found dead."

Janet reckoned that Stranger had been at the Criterion Hotel watching the strippers and the lap dancers and getting friendly with some of them by offering big tips.

They both claimed, "We were in Fortitude Valley, trying to entrap him and suss him out, when we propositioned the plain clothes policeman in an unmarked car."

They were pissed off that they were charged with soliciting and claimed the copper sort of looked like Stranger and the vehicle looked like his Ford Territory.

They then admitted, "We were off our faces and totally misjudged the situation."

They paid what was owing and were told by Carol that a specialist surveillance guy had been hired and that they would have to pay for that as well. She also advised them that they'd be best to obtain Kathryn as their solicitor, "As she is a friend of ours."

And Denise told them, "I will have a chat with the Police Prosecutor regarding your current charges as we don't want to see you imprisoned for trying to help us."

Denise and Carol both thanked them for keeping them informed of the local gossip and told them to keep pursing this area as they were in the know. Marcia and Janet were told to stay away from Stranger as he was a dangerous psychopath who would not give a second thought for their wellbeing. They both solemnly promised, then left the office.

Incorrigible those two, Carol thought, and had a feeling they would not do as they were asked as they had been in several tricky situations in the past. These girls were fearless and cheeky and would not give in as they strongly believed he had murdered their friend. They'd told us why they figured it was him. They said their friend, Shelley, had told them about him, how good looking and charming he was, how he did not take drugs or drink in excess, and how their sexual antics were becoming stranger as time went on.

Chapter Twelve

Jed knew what he had to do, that is to gather evidence against Stranger that would hold up in court. He was able to get much closer to the house Stranger occupied than Carol and Denise had. He utilised his surveillance skills and was able to take several photos of him as he went about his usual and unusual activities.

Stranger had returned to the units at Capalaba several times and appeared to be taking items from the backyard. Jed had checked the yard out during daylight hours and noticed the occupant collected frogs, and cheap items from the local discount shop. Jed followed him to Capalaba and decided to lay and wait in the victim's backyard to enable him to take a photo of Stranger in action. As he was waiting, he heard Stranger approach. He did not jump the fence as expected but rather he threw an item over the fence that came crashing through the back window of the unit. *Hell, what was that!* He saw that one of the frogs was hanging from a smashed window as it was a full moon and visibility was good. It was no longer hanging on the back wall as it had been a few days ago. The lights came on; Jed hid in the shadows behind a cupboard on the patio as a hysterical woman looked into her backyard. He waited until she moved away from the window and high tailed it out of there, noisily jumping the back fence. He nearly ran into Stranger, who was a few houses down the street laughing aloud as he watched the commotion he had caused.

Dammit, he was nearly caught by the perpetrator and was unable to get any photos or evidence of him sneaking around in the backyard. Jed casually walked the other direction and did not look back.

"That was close," he said to himself.

He had to be more careful in future about pre-empting what Stranger would do and was glad he had decided not to dress like someone from the French resistance tonight. Jed calmly walked to his car and felt the adrenalin rush through his body; he was feeling jittery and anxious and drove off as the Police arrived at the scene. He was glad he remembered the golden rule, walk don't run, and was sure he had not been identified, but one could never be sure. This guy, Stranger, was surely getting to him.

He had been hired to watch this guy for a few hours each night and became obsessed and curious and had been following him everywhere for the last month. He had lots of photos of him leaving his house dressed in camouflage gear and then appearing in high visibility clothing dressed for work. He had photographed Stranger making phone calls from different phone boxes during work hours and had watched him go to the Criterion Hotel in Buranda to watch the strippers and lap dancers. When he went to the hotel, he noticed Stranger had changed his shirt and went into the dark and dingy premises unnoticed.

Carol and Denise had told him what Janet and Marcia discovered about his visits to the Criterion Hotel as they had been following Stranger and knew a lot of the girls that worked as dancers.

They told Jed, "We have told the girls to stay away from Stranger and let the professionals follow him around and that would be you."

Jed had no trouble sneaking into the Criterion Hotel. The place was a dump, the lighting was dim, and the premises was occupied by either young blokes on the make or over-the-hill dirty old men that leered and cheered the dancers on, stuffing money into their bras and undies. To his surprise, most of the dancers were young and quite good looking. Some of the dancers were barely of age, others appeared a bit over-the-hill and worse for wear.

Jed spotted Stranger in his usual seat, right up the front, obscured by one of the poles. He was chatting to a woman about forty and looking up the crotch of one of the good-looking pole dancers, who was leaning over backwards, wearing a G-string, and showing her wares to the audience. If you could call the leering, cheering, dribbly faces before her an audience. He had to squint his eyes to enable better vision to see who Stranger was talking too and who was being very affectionate to him.

Strike a light, it looks like Janet. Blow it, he thought, *she had been told to stay away from him.*

Jed had to admit that she scrubbed up all right or was it the lighting.

Stranger stood up to leave and tucked fifty dollars into the G-string of the dancer he had been watching all night. He whispered something in Janet's ear and appeared to get her phone number. Jed stayed put and let him pass, and he then approached Janet and offered to buy her a drink.

Jed casually strolled over and asked her straight out, "Why are you talking to Stranger when Denise told you to stay away?"

She replied, looking smug, "He was chatting me up and I gave him my phone number and it's none of your business."

He told her, "Well it is my business as I'm working for Hargreaves and Plummer as an investigator. Remember them? The firm you and Marcia hired to investigate Stranger. You know they warned you about him, He's dangerous."

She shrugged her shoulders and asked him his name and then

introduced him to the dancer Stranger had been ogling all night. She was a very attractive-looking girl about twenty-four years old, long brown hair, good body, and lovely hazel eyes. She appeared to know Janet very well and told her that 'creep-features' gave her fifty dollars and asked her out for dinner.

Chapter Thirteen

He arrived at Hargreaves and Plummer's office at ten a.m. for the next meeting. This was the third report he'd given about Stranger's activities.

He informed them, "I've been working extra hours as I've had a gut feeling that this guy is up to no good."

Denise and Carol had no idea he had been doing extra hours and had no idea how they would pay for it. He had given them the surveillance work that had kept their business viable, and they knew their clients, Janet and Marcia, couldn't afford his hourly rate.

They discussed this with him, and he gave them a cunning look and said again, "I am charging mates rates and have given my current invoice to Rosslyn."

He explained, "I've been following Stranger for the last four weeks, day and night. I've become obsessed with his activities after I searched his house. illegally and found pornographic photos of women and children and have been wondering whether we should contact ANCOR."

Too right we should, they thought, but told him instead that they would have to seek legal advice as this information was illegally obtained. He added that he also found some snuff movies. He told them about the phone calls and his several visits to the Criterion Hotel. He dobbed Janet in and told Denise and Carol about the young prostitute, lap dancer come stripper, named Katherine Pierce.

Carol and Denise looked at each other and exclaimed, "We know her."

That's why Jed liked these two, they knew a lot of people who were criminals, knew a lot about them, and if they didn't know, they were good at finding things out about them.

Carol told the meeting that Pierce was a known fraudster with a drug habit. She remembered her well as she had supervised her when she was on a Probation Order. She told the meeting that Pierce was the best presented, most reliable reporter on her case load. She never re-offended or skipped a beat. Carol advised them that, when she was a parole officer, she liked to conduct random home visits without prior warning. She advised that she was surprised at the squalor and filth Katherine lived in with her young children.

She said, "The only thing I could do at the time was report this issue to child safety to enable them to check the family in case of child neglect, which is known to be the biggest risk to children."

But it reminded her of the old saying in the Probation Service, which was 'beware of the fraudster'. This is because lying and deceit are just one part of their repertoire for crime as they had many bows to draw.

Denise knew her as well and expanded on this theory. She then told the meeting about what she had found out about the victim at Capalaba, of the ongoing harassment by phone, and intimidation by stalking. Denise was thinking out aloud.

"We could probably get him for intimidating a witness and perverting the course of justice and could probably add stalking and breaching his ANCOR conditions."

She took all of Jed's photos and copies of his evidence and said matter of fact, "Leave it with me."

Denise was gorgeous when she was hot on the trail, her blue eyes sparkled, and her usual stern face lit up when she smiled. She was smiling now.

Everyone at the meeting agreed to a plan of action and to meet on a fortnightly basis from now on. After Jed left, they checked his bill he had given to Rosslyn. He had given her a blank piece of paper, God love him.

Chapter Fourteen

Stranger had the feeling he was being watched. *That can't be right,* he thought, *as I am the watcher. Hell, I'm getting paranoid.*

He no longer had to explain his activities to his parole officer. He remembered the time he told his parole officer that he was in a new relationship. She told him to bring her to his next appointment. He had no idea that she was going to challenge him about his new relationship and wanted his new girlfriend to tell her what offences he was on parole for. She had, of course, no idea and was unable to give any details as he had not told her that he was a sex offender that had been convicted of murdering his last partner. No problem in ceasing that relationship as she was a plain and desperate woman that was obliging in his sex games. Due to this fact, he had not bothered obtaining or maintaining a relationship and began to utilise prostitutes to meet his needs.

He began to think about his fantasies and felt the urge to groom another victim. He felt he had to get rid of all pornographic and child abuse DVD's, videos, and photos. He knew his ANCOR officer had not contacted him or made any surprise visits for a while and could expect one any day. He decided that he would get rid of any incriminating material today. It was a feeling he had that someone was watching him and had been inside his house. *God that was fun the other night*, he thought, *the frog flying through the window, what a laugh.*

The guy walking down the street behind the flats played on his mind. *What was he doing at that hour of the morning?* He knew he'd have to dump his computer as they (the police) could retrieve deleted files.

He started thinking about his visits to the Criterion Hotel and decided to give Janet a call. This would enable him to get back into practice with the conning and manipulation of his next victim. He'd seen her around and knew she was on the game. She wasn't bad looking for her age, dressed well, and was fairly entertaining and friendly when she gave him her contact number. He decided he would start with her and would practice his romancing skills. He would take his time and pretend he was interested in her and her life. She looked like she was a drug user but not a heavily addicted one. He knew his real interest was in the younger pole dancer, now that was a good sort, he'd like to know her better. She was the perfect-looking victim.

Thinking of victims, he pondered his legal matter. He knew Kathryn Harrison was a damned good solicitor with a good reputation for getting charges dropped or dismissed. Her last explanation at court that legal aid had not been approved and the Police had not supplied a brief of evidence gave him some hope. He knew this happens when the police can't get enough evidence to prosecute and started to believe his plan to intimidate the victim's mother was working well. He had the feeling, however, that he needed to be more vigilant.

He phoned Janet and made a date to take her to lunch at a Mexican eatery at Capalaba. She seemed pleased to hear from him.

Chapter Fifteen

Business at Hargreaves and Plummer was picking up due to obtaining extra work from Work Cover and Centrelink. They'd been hired to investigate workplace and Centrelink fraud. They were good at networking. Carol disliked the notion of networking when she was a parole officer as she thought it was a middle-class idea and believed those that networked in most cases were crawling up the boss's arse. How things change when you're self-employed. She used all her contacts at Work Cover and Centrelink and her efforts had started to pay off in obtaining work for their private investigation firm.

Denise, on the other hand, had maintained contact within the police service since her retirement. She'd trained the current police prosecutor and found out from him that the police brief for Stranger was not progressing well. The complainant had withdrawn the complaint and the police were not sure whether they would have enough evidence to prosecute and were considering withdrawing the charge against him at this time.

She'd contacted the ANCOR Officer in Stranger's area and told him about the information she had obtained from Jed Atkins' surveillance. It appeared that Stranger may have breached his order by having pornographic photos and information of child abuse sites on his computer. Constable Jones indicated he was the only officer available at the moment and was inundated by new court orders, ANCOR registrations, and court briefs to prepare for other ANCORS that had breached their orders. He could not promise to check this information out but would try.

God, this is frustrating, thought Denise, *glad I'm no longer on the job. If the public knew how understaffed and overworked police officers were, they would be outraged. The new recruits barely cover the stress leave, the suspensions from duty, and the overall depletion rate from resignations.*

If they knew Corrective Services placed a lot of (Serious Violent Offenders)SVO, paedophiles and sex offenders in a halfway house near the prison gates as they are unable to house them in the community, they'd be further outraged, she thought.

When the Government introduced the new sex offender legislation, the Chief Justice advised at the time that these offenders should not be allowed to congregate or associate with each other. Due to the inability to place them in the community they fester and discuss their urges, offences and think it's a huge laugh. If the public only knew, it's become a huge not in my backyard (NIMBY) issue to be bought out again at the next election, boost police numbers that doesn't cover resignations or suspensions.

Carol heard Denise venting and laughed, "Don't you remember the good old days when police corruption was the norm? In New South Wales, there was graffiti in Woolloomooloo that said Robert Askin (New South Wales Premier) loves Lora Norda. Not to worry, mate, we have a lot of work and surveillance to do and need to allocate who does what job."

Rosslyn was allocated the Work Cover job and appeared to be happy to be able to do something constructive as she'd been sitting on her arse for the last two months watching security tapes of thieves. She decided to take Richmond on her surveillance as cover. The alleged fraudster had worked for the company for three weeks when he had allegedly injured his back and has been receiving compensation for the last three years. Work Cover believed he was not incapacitated and wanted film and evidence of his activities. Rosslyn was over the moon; she was a good photographer and liked making short films in her free time.

Carol took the Centrelink job; she was tasked with checking out a single mother who was suspected of claiming benefits for herself and children. Centrelink were not sure whether she was working or whether she was claiming another benefit. Carol kept thinking, *beware of the fraudster.*

Chapter Sixteen

Jed had been watching Stranger for over a month. He'd stopped going to Capalaba at night and there was not a lot of activity to report. The only exception was when ANCOR and police arrived to check his premises. They appeared to have a search warrant and took several items away, including a computer, but did not appear very happy. On the other hand, Stranger appeared calm and not worried about what was found. Stranger went to the Criterion Hotel a few times and looked like he was enjoying himself, chatting up chicks and showing particular interest in Katherine Pierce, the young dancer.

He was seen with Autumn, aka Janet Miller, taking her and her two sons shopping, to the movies, and to a Mexican restaurant. He appeared to be the perfect man, chatting, laughing and generally sociable, kind and patient with the children. Janet appeared to be enjoying his company and was relaxed and engaging with her attention focussed on him. He did not stay overnight and appeared to be grooming the family, popping around with gifts of computer games for the boys and something nice for their mother.

Janet and Marcia had been friends, sometimes lovers, for over twenty-five years. They'd changed their names to Autumn and Winter due to Janet being born in March and Winter, aka Marcia, being born in July. They'd both had the same parole officer who at first insisted on calling them Janet and Marcia but finally capitulated to their pseudo names. Janet in her youth was what they called 'drop dead gorgeous'. She had amazing blue eyes which she highlighted with heavy eye makeup, that black-eyed wanton look. She had a body to die for. Marcia, on the other hand, was good looking with hazel eyes, good complexion, heavier build, and was about five feet seven. Janet was a petite five foot four and had everyone, boys and girls, chasing her. They both had the personalities that made whoever they were speaking to or associating with feel special. However, the years and lifestyle choices had given them a harder look, and in their youth, they were legendary to the amount of drugs they could consume, usually speed, marijuana, and alcohol. They'd both met in Sydney and worked as prostitutes out of a famous house in Foveaux Street, Surry Hills. They moved to Queensland about fifteen years ago when Janet had her first child. Even though they did not live together, they remained firm friends that could rely on each other in times of need.

They met for lunch at the Capalaba Shopping Centre. Janet told Marcia that she'd been going out with Stranger, and she felt they had been wrong about him.

She told Marcia, "He is a perfect gentleman who has taken me and the kids out and bought them presents, including a computer. He also shows lots of patience and kindness when my boys fight over the Wii game."

She reckoned that she could tell if he was going to be tricky.

"Come off it," said Marcia. "This is exactly how Shelley described her new man."

Marcia had always been the sensible one of the two. Janet insisted he had not been trying to get into her pants, was a good kisser, and showed genuine interest in her and her kids. She could not be swayed, even though her best friend tried to talk some sense into her. But Marcia knew from her friend's past behaviour, she was not someone to be told or take advice.

Stranger thought things were going well. Hell, ANCOR had checked his premises and took away some items he knew would not be incriminating. Intuition is a good thing; Janet's kids loved the new computer with the games on it. He thought his romancing skills were still above average and his show of patience with the kids seemed to impress their mother.

"Slow and steady, that's the way to do it, that always sucks in the lonely ones. Show a little tenderness and kindness in this cruel, cruel world. Shit, I'm funny. Go home to wank and fantasise about destroying the little family, no one will care what happens to them. Then, of course, this will be good practice for the ultimate goal, to get that chick at the Criterion Hotel eating out of my hand. God, I won't be able to sleep tonight due to the erotic fantasies I'll be having. Once again, the coppers have nothing on me. Course, I'm a genius manipulator and far too smart for anyone to catch me."

He went on to laughing his head off – or one of his heads off.

Chapter Seventeen

Rosslyn and Richmond set off in the campervan to enable them to conduct the surveillance of the Work Cover job. After she'd set up her camera equipment, they waited down the road from the nominated address. During times when there appeared to be no movement from the house, she and Richmond went for walks around the neighbourhood to enable them to get closer to the house. The house itself was a modest fibro house in a suburb known for its low socioeconomic residents. The lawn appeared to be recently cut, but there was a fair amount of junk in the yard, broken cars and other machinery. They'd been there for a week and had seen the occupant twice, hobbling to the letterbox with the aid of a walking stick, dressed in a high visibility shirt and jeans.

Rosslyn discussed the lack of progress with Carol when she got home that night. They both thought it was peculiar for someone to wear work clothes around the house. Then the penny dropped. If this person is allegedly pouring concrete, they knew those jobs started early in the morning as concrete needs to be poured before the heat of the day. They decided it would be more probable that this guy would leave for work between five and six o'clock in the morning. They decided they would have to set up their surveillance early next week as the previous week's photos were totally useless to them.

Richmond had settled in at their house and had a huge yard and kennel and was allowed inside at night. Rosslyn started to take him to work and maintained his training and discipline.

They'd become inseparable. Carol would molly coddle him at night, and they would sit on the couch watching Inspector Rex.

Rosslyn had noticed that Richmond took a dislike to certain individuals. He liked all women but was very tricky to the point of biting men with beer bellies who dressed in King Gee singlets and stubby shorts; he also disliked drunks and dry drunks. She wasn't sure whether it was the way they walked or whether it was their demeanour. But Richmond always snapped at them if they came too close and had to be kept on a short lead whenever this type of bloke approached them on the street.

Carol had taped all the Inspector Rex series over the years and would happily watch them again with Richmond curled up on her lap.

Rosslyn and Richmond arrived at their surveillance of the Work Cover job at five a.m. the following Monday morning. By the look of the pair of them, they did not like getting up this early as they both looked dishevelled and were feeling grumpy. There was no movement from the house until mid-morning, when a car arrived and pulled into the driveway. The driver went inside and left an hour later. Rosslyn heard them discussing tomorrow's job. She decided to leave and take Richmond for a walk before returning to the office at Capalaba. They returned the next day to observe the occupant leave unaided at five o'clock in the morning. She took photos of him getting into his car and followed him, maintaining a safe distance behind. Fifteen minutes later, he arrived at his destination. Rosslyn pulled up two doors down and set up her equipment. Lights, camera, action. He proceeded to unload a cement mixer from the back of a trailer and mixed the concrete. She filmed and watched him and his friend pour and level concrete for the next three hours. She had some good footage of the work in progress, including the target on his hands and knees levelling the concrete as quick has he could do it. They completed the job by noon and packed up and left. They'd been laying a concrete driveway. Rosslyn returned to the office to check her photos and footage and was really pleased with her efforts. Richmond was pleased to be with Rosslyn as they returned to the office in a buoyant mood.

When they arrived back at the office, the fortnightly meeting was in progress. Jed and Denise reported little progress during the last fortnight. Carol advised that she was having trouble obtaining good photographic evidence on her Centrelink fraudster. She told the meeting that Centrelink wanted two families followed as they were not sure which one was the alleged guilty party. She admitted that her photography skills were not good, it was difficult to obtain a clear shot, and it was hard to differentiate between the families as they were similar in appearance. Rosslyn entered and downloaded her photos and film of her morning's surveillance. Everyone present was gobsmacked as the photos and film looked like a professional job. The fraudster and his workmate were clearly identifiable, along with their actions. The meeting ended more upbeat, and it was decided there and then that Rosslyn would be the official photo-movie maker for Hargreaves and Plummer. Rosslyn was chuffed and very pleased with her efforts, she did explain this had been her hobby for the last twenty years and that she'd spent good money on equipment. This hobby was a passion, not only a skill.

They agreed that Rosslyn would follow-up her case with more footage and then assist Carol in obtaining some footage of her Centrelink case. There was a general buzz of excitement after the meeting after Rosslyn's surveillance film was shown. There was a feeling they could now supply clear evidence in the cases they were pursuing.

Chapter Eighteen

Carol, Rosslyn, and Richmond, set off early the following Monday. Their plan was to check the Work Cover job early and then attend the Centrelink job. They knew that if the concreter did not leave early, it was probable he would stay at home all day. It was a half an hour drive between locations.

The Centrelink fraudster resided in a beach side suburb and left home at eight o'clock in the morning and went to work at a financial institution after dropping her children at childcare. The other woman appeared to attend TAFE three days a week after dropping her children at a residential address. Carol explained that the fraudster had given both addresses to Centrelink and when they called her in for a review, she would use the excuse that one of her children was sick and could not attend therefore putting off her appointment until another time. She told Rosslyn that both women and children were similar in age and appearance and their job was to identify the correct person for Centrelink. They decided to conduct surveillance of the three households for another fortnight.

Carol noted the Work Cover fraudster was easy to watch compared to the women. He either hobbled around with the aid of a walking stick at home or moved freely when pouring concrete. They had obtained more footage of him laying down formwork for concrete slabs for houses, mixing and pouring concrete. They were happy with the evidence they had accumulated over the last few weeks. Carol surmised that his walking stick was a prop he used for the benefit of his neighbours or anyone that knew him at the local shops. On the other hand, both women and families proved more difficult to observe due to how they moved.

Rosslyn set up her equipment at the first address. They observed a well-dressed woman and her children leave the house and get into the car very quickly. It was hard to get a good shot as they were obscured by the garden and they were unable to get closer to them. Both families had the requisite golden retriever dog that added to the confusion and dilemma of a good shot. They decided to concentrate on the women as they had, in their minds, satisfactorily completed the Work Cover job. To get closer to the families, Richmond was taken for a walk with Carol as Rosslyn tried to obtain some good photos and footage. Thank God they had a dog; Richmond made a beeline towards both families' retrievers while Carol played the part of a ditzy dog owner trying to get her dog back. As a result, Carol was able to chat to both women amicably about dogs and children. She was good at conversation and obtaining information from people. A few prompts and let them talk. Richmond was on his best behaviour, obedient, lovely with the kids, and nice to the other dogs. She'd told the women that she'd just moved into the neighbourhood to enable her to walk the dog past their homes at other times. For the first time, Rosslyn was able to get clear shots of both families. They were of similar ages and builds, Rosslyn's shots showed significant differences that Carol's photography had been unable to do. They decided to change their ruse. Instead of following their subjects to and from work or TAFE, they would engage them in conversation when walking the dog.

Richmond loved his new job, loved going for walks, and proved to be very sociable with other dogs and children. Carol was terrific in engaging strangers in conversation. She chatted with the first family and Richmond showed the children his tricks. Roll over, bang your dead, through the tunnel; the children found him very entertaining as their dog had a limited repertoire. Carol found out the woman was separated from her husband and worked in finance. Her name was Carolyn, the boy's name was Todd, and her daughter's name was Amber. She was well-dressed and usually wore designer suits or designer sports attire. She was well-spoken and reserved in conversation, she was pleasant enough but she did not come across as very friendly. Rosslyn got some good clean shots of her and her family.

The second family were in a similar situation in that the woman, Caroline, was separated from her partner and her son, Rod, and daughter, Annie, were of a similar age and appearance to Carolyn's family. Caroline, however, was gregarious and chatty, appeared to live in designer sportswear, track pants, t-shirts, and hoodies. She told Carol that she was on a single mothers' benefit and was doing hairdressing at TAFE as part of her job ready activities.

She said, "I have recently escaped from a destructive, violent relationship and that's why I keep to myself. The only support I have is my mother, who minds the children before and after school and when I attend my hairdressing course at the TAFE."

She was animated and expressive when discussing herself and family and had piercings in her nose and ears. Rosslyn obtained some very clear footage, and it was obvious that they were two separate identities.

Once they obtained good footage, Carol and Rosslyn decided to focus on Carolyn and her activities and reported the differences to Centrelink. The case manager, an investigator at Centrelink, gave them permission and approved payment for the evidence and footage they had obtained. They followed Carolyn for another fortnight and identified that she was working fulltime and obtaining benefits under false pretences. Centrelink advised they would be pursuing and prosecuting her in the near future and thanked Hargreaves and Plummer for the work they had done.

Chapter Nineteen

The next meeting at Hargreaves and Plummer was very positive and everyone was in a good mood. Carol advised about the successful work completed for Work Cover and Centrelink, who had advised them that they would give them further cases to investigate in the future.

Denise reported that she'd contacted Police Prosecutions and ANCOR, who had indicated they may not have enough evidence to prosecute Stranger as the witness had withdrawn the complaint and the seized computer had no incriminating evidence on the hard drive. The police felt that they could not obtain a conviction and were considering neto-ing the brief.

Denise stated, "I have contacted Kathryn and Margo and have arranged a meeting at the Coffee Club at Cleveland for tomorrow at two p.m."

Jed told the meeting, "Stranger continues to go out at night to Fortitude Valley and the Criterion Hotel, is still seeing Janet and taking her and her boys out for outings."

He advised, "I am feeling frustrated due to the lack of progress, but I am convinced Stranger is up to something".

They reviewed Rosslyn's footage and photos from the fraud cases and everyone, including Richmond, was appreciative. He appeared to know he was on some of the footage and barked and wagged his tail when he was on film.

"A real Inspector Rex," exclaimed Carol as everyone laughed and rolled their eyes.

Carol and Denise felt very positive about their business enterprise and were happy with the people they had enlisted or hired to help.

Denise and Carol reflected on meetings they had attended in their previous occupations where, if an opinion was asked for and offered, it was totally ignored with a 'my way or the highway' approach to management. Here at Hargreaves and Plummer, opinions were sought with the view of changing tactics if something was not achieving the result that was wanted. All had agreed to change tactics and put some pressure on Stranger.

By the end of the meeting, new strategies began evolving and everyone was participating in the discussion as part of a team. It was agreed that Jed would take Rosslyn and sometimes Richmond on his trips to Fortitude Valley and the Criterion Hotel. They would utilise Richmond on an as needed basis. Rosslyn would try to get clear shots of who Stranger was talking to on his night-time jaunts to see if they could be identified through their sources within the Police and Parole Service.

Carol added that, "parole officers are good at identifying people who they have supervised as they are the only ones who have a lot of contact with their clients over the years."

The older officers were particularly good and have incredible memories for names and faces that they have developed over years due to dealing with the same clients over and over again.

Denise and Carol would attend the meeting with Kathryn and Margo to outline their plans and what sort of assistance may be needed. They were also going to contact Janet and Marcia as they wanted to find out what they were up to. The girls were due in this week to pay their fees and they were concerned about Janet continuing her friendship with Stranger. They were concerned for her safety.

Chapter Twenty

Stranger knew there was a reason he did not drink alcohol. He nearly lost it last night. He'd been playing the perfect gentleman and happy families with the old hooker and felt comfortable in her company. Even though she had two kids, she kept a tidy and clean house that surprised him as it suited his need for control and order. She'd smoke a bit of pot and have a few bourbons after her kids went to bed but never got out of control as far as he could tell.

Hell, he'd got out of control last night. He had planned to seduce her to further the relationship to one of trust. She'd offered him a can of Jim Beam, and before he knew it, she was seducing him. He did not like the feeling of losing control and almost choked her when his fantasies became mixed or blurred with reality. She had the wherewithal to knee him in the groin as she was gasping for air.

God she was a good sport, he thought. She accepted the behaviour as just one of those things that got out of hand. That's the good thing about experienced hookers, they are not easily shocked, like water off a duck's back.

He left on good terms, and she'd told him, "Don't worry about it, mate, shit happens."

When he left her house, he went straight home. He was disappointed that he was unable to control his desires and his alcohol use. He remembered what his old parole officer told him about alcoholism when he boasted to her that he did not take drugs but enjoyed a few drinks occasionally. But he had stopped drinking as he could not control his behaviour when intoxicated. She'd told him at the time, as far as she was concerned alcohol was a dangerous drug, not only harmful to physical health but harmful to mental health. She lent him a copy of the original Alcoholics Anonymous book to take home and read to gain a better understanding of himself. He wasn't much of a reader, but sections of that book described him perfectly. The first section on alcoholic personalities was very informative; he was a perfectionist, liked things ordered, and was extremely clean and tidy in his habits, almost obsessional. *Well, not almost*, he thought, *I am obsessed with order*. As he looked around his house, fastidious, everything had its place, even his drawers where he kept his clothing was ordered, neat and tidy, no item of clothing was ever shoved haphazardly away. His clothes were all folded and regimental. He thought at the time it was because he was institutionalised from being in prison but realised after reading the book that he had always been tidy. That's probably why he fitted into the prison regime. The definition of his style of alcohol use determined that he was an alcoholic as he had an allergic reaction to alcohol. Hell, he counted his drinks last night; paced himself and drank no more than six cans of bourbons, the same as Janet. He remembered his parole officer telling him that if you want to stop at four drinks you can, but once you pass that level, alcohol takes over and then you can't stop. She'd also told him about dry drunks. He'd never heard of the term but there was a section in the book advising that alcoholics who were medically defined as allergic to alcohol could cease all use but maintain the personality traits. These traits were described as being perfectionists, picky and nit-picky with others if they don't have the same values for order and control. That is, as his old parole officer used to say, still an arsehole but a sober one. He thought about this and reflected on the wisdom of what she was trying to get him to understand.

When he thought about last night, he did not feel guilty or sad. He realised his only thought was whether she would tell anyone or report the matter to police. But she assured him that she would not do anything of the sort as she felt responsible for his behaviour as she was the one who plied him with alcohol when she knew he did not drink. *He'd phone her to make sure that things were still good*. His thoughts drifted to his fantasy of grooming the younger lap dancer and her children. Hell, Janet was not going to be his next victim, she was too well known and had quite a few friends that would miss her. In reality, she was a practice run on how to hone seduction skills and groom a family, to become a trusted, indispensable friend and father figure. He took the tattered photo from his wallet; he was a father but had never seen his daughter and fantasied on who she was and how successful she had become in life.

He phoned Janet, she was cool but told him, "It might be a good idea not to see each other again."

He agreed and was relieved he did not have to see her again. He was not sorry but felt a bit embarrassed as he could not really remember last night. He began to think about his next victim, the lap dancer. He realised he was becoming obsessed with having her under his control and now felt confident that he could charm and manipulate her as he had done with Janet. She should be easier to manipulate as she was much younger, at least twenty-four. *He'd have to spruce himself up a bit as he thought he was looking his age.* He thought that, with a makeover, he could pass for thirty-five. The more he thought about his long-term goal, he developed a plan to work on himself, physically, and then set his plan in action for this next victim. *No more trolling in Fortitude Valley, he would befriend her at the Criterion Hotel where she worked.* He felt confident after he had spoken with his solicitor and had been advised his matter may not proceed due to lack of evidence. *No worries then*, he thought. Always the clever one, he went to bed laughing his head off again. *Got to stop that, even my own laughter is giving me the creeps.*

Chapter Twenty-One

Marcia phoned Hargreaves and Plummer and left a message for either Denise or Carol to return her call. Denise returned her call as soon as she arrived and arranged for the girls to come into the office at eleven a.m. Marcia had told Denise about the ligature marks on Janet's neck. Between them, it was decided that Carol would talk to Janet alone as she knew her better than Denise and they thought she may be more open with her.

Janet arrived early without Marcia. Carol intercepted her and took her into her office, offering morning tea. As Carol made the coffee and put some biscuits on a plate, Janet sat opposite her desk.

Carol chatted about her boys and asked, "How are your boys going at school?"

Janet replied, "They both doing as well as can be expected, they both have behavioural and learning problems."

Janet looked relaxed and chatted away. As Carol was observing her, she noticed the scarf around her neck. She became more animated and Carol saw the bruises on her neck.

"Shit, Janet, what's that on your neck, a hickey?"

Janet's hand went immediately to her neck as Carol said, "That's not a hickey."

Janet then appeared flustered but continued chatting away and told her that, "Stranger nearly choked me last night, but it was my fault as I'd been goading him and deserved it."

Carol was gobsmacked, she'd known Janet for at least ten

years and knew whatever she said to her would make no difference. She would never report anything to police that personally involved her as it was against her criminal ethic. On the other hand, she didn't mind dobbing in others if it could be kept anonymous. There were some offences Janet did not like, she did not like ice manufacturers and drug dealing that involved children or extreme violence, including murder. Carol knew this as she'd told her in the past.

Janet flippantly said, "I am over Stranger, and I won't be seeing him again."

Carol was not that sure as she'd heard this type of statement before and knew she was extremely strong-willed and generally did what she liked when she liked without considering the consequences. Carol figured out long ago that this was part of the criminal mindset; they only worried if they were caught. Otherwise, it was business as usual. Carol considered that it was also part of the drug culture; they never really grew up, real Peter Pans and Wendy's.

By the time Marcia arrived, Janet and Carol were onto their second cup of coffee. The atmosphere in the room took on a certain chill after Marcia entered the office as she was really pissed off at her friend. Carol left the room to let the girls sort out what was going on between them.

She got Denise aside and told her, "The situation with Janet is hopeless, she will not report or incriminate Stranger as she feels she deserved nearly getting garrotted."

They both knew that this ideation was common amongst women that were used to abusive relationships and unfortunately common for working girls, whose trade was made of rough stuff.

When Denise and Carol returned to Carol's office, the girls seemed to have sorted out their issues and were chatting away about their next shopping expedition. They shut up as soon as they entered. Both Carol and Denise gave each other the look, they knew they'd almost overheard a criminal plan to go shoplifting or obtaining five finger discounts. They had other things to think about and the reality was they could do nothing about it.

The girls paid what was owed on their account and both swore off Stranger and promised not to meddle again. Denise read them the riot act in no uncertain terms.

She told them, "You can't afford any more criminal charges with your prior records; the Soliciting and Drug offences are proving difficult to remove and you'd have no hope if you are charged and convicted with another offence."

"You'd both go to prison because of your past records," Denise told them. "You two better back off Stranger, Hargreaves and Plummer will take care of him and we do not need your involvement or help in any way."

But she added, "We would listen to any information you have obtained from others."

The girls promised to pass on any information, promised to be good, and that they would stay away from Stranger. They then doddled off to go shopping.

Chapter Twenty-Two

After they left Hargreaves and Plummer, Janet and Marcia decided to go to the pub for lunch. During lunch, they discussed their legal situation, and both agreed with Denise that they would be in trouble if they were convicted with further offences. So, for the time being, they decided not to go shopping as they really did not need any more sports attire. They realised they had got away from A-Mart Sports quite a few times without being caught and knew every time they went shoplifting there was a risk of being caught, but it was more exciting than buying stuff they did not need. They hoped Denise would be able to have the current charges dropped as they knew it was likely they would either go to prison or be sentenced to Court Ordered Parole. They both agreed that they needed another community-based order like a hole in the head. Christ, they'd be unable to leave the State without permission, would have to attend drug counselling and submit to urine tests. That would be a real pain in the arse, they'd rather do the time. But prison was a hassle as Janet would have to have her previous old man look after the kids he did not like. He was the father of one of her boys and only just tolerated her eldest son, Jayden, who was fourteen and could be a bit mouthy. They decided not to thieve but continue dealing a bit of pot to finance their lifestyle.

Janet, aka Autumn, told Marcia, aka Winter, what happened with Stranger and said, "I will not be seeing him again as I've seen another side of him that was not very nice, creepy even."

She said, "He had been considerate, kind, and appeared interested in her and her boys, or so she thought."

She told Marcia, "I only gave him a few bourbons and he appeared effected and by the time he finished his six pack, he was pretty pissed."

She then said, "We tumbled off to the bedroom and I was feeling horny and just about pulled his clothes off as he appeared pretty keen on the idea."

Janet told Marcia, "I had the scarf on I had worn that day and did not have time to get fully undressed before he pounced on me."

She reckoned, "I had been leading him on all night and, after all, a root's a root. I did not expect the world's best lover, but I did not expect the mad rooter that banged way as hard as he could. As he came, I saw a terrible, ugly looking face that was full of anger as he grabbed hold of the scarf around my neck."

"Well, what could a girl do but knee him in the goolies. Christ," she told Marcia. "I thought I was going to die."

Marcia did not say much at all; she could have said 'I told you so' but restrained herself. What she did say assured Janet that her friend would always be her friend and would keep her disclosure confidential.

Marcia hugged Janet and told her, "You are a first class idiot and I still love you."

They then had a good laugh about all the mad rooters they had known.

"If you want a handsome, debonair, thoughtful lover, read a Barbara Cartland book, it's better than the arseholes we seem to attract."

They decided they were right about him all along and felt that they had to help Hargreaves and Plummer in their investigation. They wondered how they could assist without having Denise Hargreaves rip their bloody arms off, as she almost promised to do if they 'meddled' again. They knew they could not entice him with drugs or alcohol, and after Janet's experience, neither of them wanted to seduce him as they now feared that he was as dangerous as Carol had tried to tell them. What they could do was warn Katherine Pierce but knew she'd probably take as much notice of the warning as Janet had done. They both knew Janet had been lucky and knew Katherine Pierce was twenty years younger than them and thought she knew it all. Well, you can't put an old head on young shoulders, but they would certainly try to warn her off Stranger.

Chapter Twenty-Three

Denise and Carole met Margo and Kathryn at the Coffee Club at Cleveland. Denise told everyone what she'd found out from her mates in the police service. They probably would withdraw the charges against Stranger. Kathryn confirmed this information as she had not received the brief and had passed on this information to Stranger. He was pleased and thanked her for her expertise, as if she'd had something to do with it. Kathryn advised that if the police withdrew, she would have to withdraw the legal aid application, which had not been approved to date. She said the girls' legal aid application was still pending, and she would keep everyone informed on its progress.

Margo had followed up on Pierce and Stranger using her contacts by asking other offenders about these two individuals. She said that Pierce is currently under supervision on a two-year Probation Order for credit card fraud and was supervised at the Brisbane Office as she lived in Morningside. Her case worker had told Margo that she was employed as a dancer and kept all her scheduled weekly appointments. Margo supplied her address. She also advised that Stranger was not liked by the criminal fraternity, who claimed he was a loner and a know-it-all, and no one likes a smart arse. Criminals don't like sex offenders either and no one had a good word to say about him.

Denise told everyone what Hargreaves and Plummer had been up to and they discussed how they could put some pressure on Stranger. It was agreed they would have ANCOR do unscheduled home visits.

Margo suggested, "I could get Kathryn Pierce's case manager to put some pressure on her to confirm her employment and apply to the courts to have drug testing as a condition on her order, as it is not a current condition."

She added, "I could also have the Probation Service conduct random home visits to find out her living situation."

As Carol had indicated, she would be suspicious of her activities as she had supervised her in the past and knew she could present well while her life was in chaos.

Carol thanked Margo and Kathryn for their assistance and said, "We will continue our surveillance on Stranger and will also follow Pierce to find out what she is up to and who she is in contact with in her spare time and will pass on any relevant information."

They enjoyed meeting at the Coffee Club as the food and the coffee was always great. They agreed to see each other again in a month's time. Margo looked her usual frazzled self but had a sophisticated demeanour as she was well bought up and schooled. She could present as a bit posh but had a wicked sense of humour and good dress sense. Kathryn Harrison was always open and friendly and appeared to live in designer suits. Carol and Denise, on the other hand, were in casual clothes and had an 'I'm on holiday look', hard to pick them from their previous working lives. Denise now had a radical hair cut that would not have been accepted when she was in the Police Service. Her hair was a bit spiky, with a short back and sides.

She claimed she felt younger and more vital and looked it, she said, "My husband hates the look, but not to worry, I love it and that's all that matters."

She had also lost a bit of weight, as had Carol, since their retirement. Carol had her hair cut short but not as radical as Denise. Denise was dressed trendy casual, Carol looked like she had just left the beach or returned from a camping trip. Both looked entirely different, relaxed, and happy, with a carefree attitude. Aside from their appearance, they maintained that they were serious about nailing Stranger for something.

Chapter Twenty-Four

Jed arrived at Hargreaves and Plummer at nine thirty a.m. They had agreed to meet to discuss their new strategy of applying pressure on Stranger and Pierce. Denise started the discussion and advised that ANCOR would put some pressure on him by conducting more checks on a regular basis.

She added, "General duties police will pull him over in his car whenever possible to further our cause. They will check his driver's licence, his sobriety, and conduct searches of his vehicle. That usually makes criminals antsy, which will be the purpose of their checks."

Jed was insistent, "I am sure I saw child porn and other incriminating evidence on Stranger's computer. I can't understand why there was nothing on the hard drive of the computer the police seized."

Then they discussed how and when they would obtain photo images and film where possible of their suspects. Jed explained he had not been able to follow Stranger for a few nights as he had other obligations to his family. They decided that Rosslyn, Carol and Richmond, would use the same strategy when conducting surveillance on Pierce as they had used on the Centrelink fraudster. It was further agreed that Jed and Rosslyn would follow Stranger if he left his house at night.

They arrived at Katherine Pierce's Morningside address the next morning. They got out of the campervan and Carol proceeded to take Richmond for a walk as Rosslyn set up her cameras. The house was set back off the street, the garden was unkempt, and it was hard to see into the house due to the overgrown garden beds and long grass. There was no movement until noon. They watched Katherine Pierce leave her house with two young children in tow. They all looked well-dressed, clean and tidy. Carol and Rosslyn decided not to follow her as they knew she had an appointment with her probation officer. They decided to have a look around the house because she was not at home.

Richmond ran into the yard as instructed and went around the back of the property. Carol knocked on the front door to check whether anyone was home. Her excuse if there was someone home would be that she was retrieving her naughty dog. No one answered the door. They proceeded to look through windows. The place was furnished well, with good quality television and white goods, Game Boys, and lots of video games for the kids. In amongst the expensive furniture were piles of rubbish and dirty clothes. The place was a tip. The kitchen was filthy, with rotting food in the sink and on the floor. Carol spied a bong on the coffee table in the lounge room next to a mull bowl. Richmond was barking and Rosslyn went to see what he was barking at. In amongst the weeds were several small marijuana plants. Rosslyn took photos of the plants and what could be seen through the windows of the house and called Richmond back. They set off in the camper to return to the office to decide how they would use this information. They would return the next day as Rosslyn had to go with Jed that night to follow Stranger.

Jed and Rosslyn were in position when Stranger arrived home from work. He had a certain spring in his step and went inside for an hour. He left his house dressed in trendy sportswear, clean and showered. They followed him to his local gym where he worked out for an hour. Rosslyn took a few photos while Jed made enquiries about joining the gym. He had a look around to see what Stranger was doing, he appeared to be working his core, toning up his upper body and stomach. *Vain bastard*, thought Jed, looking down at his flabby tummy. He knew he was a bit out of shape as he had given up his gym activities over a year ago when he tore a tendon in his leg. *Might as well join up*, he thought, and this would allow him to follow him legitimately to the gym. When Stranger left the gym, he showered again after his workout. *Boy this guy is a clean freak*, thought Rosslyn. They followed him to a newly opened men's makeover shop in Cleveland. He went inside for over an hour and came out looking pleased with himself. He then went home and did not leave until the next morning, when he left for work in his usual high visibility clothes.

Rosslyn and Carol followed Pierce for a week after deciding to let Jed follow Stranger alone as Rosslyn was not up to double shifts.

Rosslyn took photos of people coming and going from the Morningside address and Pierce's lifestyle became clear. She had a regular female visitor that looked after her kids when she worked at the Criterion Hotel. Her shifts had changed; she was now working from midday till night.

Carol went into the Criterion Hotel to see the lunch time crowd drooling over their beers and the flexible pole dancers, another world entirely to the one outside. Carol could not believe there were blokes, and some ladies, who would attend such activities during daylight hours. As she was thinking this to herself, she spotted Janet and Marcia arriving. They both bought bourbons and went to sit where the dancers had their break. When Pierce had her break from dancing, she went to the table where the girls were sitting. The girls appeared to be having an in-depth, animated conversation with her. Carol wondered what they were talking about and decided to call the girls into the office for a chat. She left without being seen and told Rosslyn what was going on inside the Criterion Hotel.

Carol had been unable to engage Pierce with the dog routine as her children appeared scared of dogs and were shy and reserved. They weren't the type of children who would talk to strangers, as they had been schooled by their mother, a welfare recipient, not to talk to strangers. She was always wary of child welfare and had told her children not to annoy or talk to anyone they did not know. Their mother was annoyed that the dog was not on a lead.

Chapter Twenty-Five

Rosslyn and Jed followed Stranger after work. His routine had changed, and he attended the gym daily, went to the men's parlour once a week, where he bought supplements and men's grooming and hair removal products. He also attended a clinic that offered Botox face lifts. Jed went to both places to find out what was on offer.

He told Rosslyn, "Stranger appears to be working on improving his looks and appearance."

This was confirmed when they followed him to a men's clothing shop where he bought good quality suits, shirts, and shoes. Rosslyn had been busy with her camera.

That night, after midnight, he left his house to cruise Fortitude Valley. He had not been near the Criterion Hotel for a month. He drove into town again on Friday night. They followed him into Fortitude Valley and could see him chatting to a woman on the corner opposite the big intersection where they were parked. Rosslyn could not get a clear shot as they were too far away. Rosslyn saw the person he was talking to get into his car and took a photo.

She said to Jed, "We'd better follow him as he has just picked up someone."

As Jed went to move on to follow them, a policewoman stood out in front of him with a 'Stop, police' sign. They had not noticed the random drug and alcohol test unit set up as they were watching and concentrating on Stranger. Jed spoke into the alcoholmeter, was swabbed for illicit drugs, and had to wait a few minutes for the result of the tests and licence and registration checks before he was allowed to go. Police were checking all vehicles that entered Fortitude Valley. Rosslyn saw Stranger's first left turn and they took off after him. As they took the next left, they realised he was nowhere in sight. They had lost him. They drove around the area for the next half hour and decided he was gone so they returned to his address. He was not there and had not returned by mid-morning. They went home after an exhausting, non-productive night.

They would return the next night. They watched his place of residence all weekend and he did not return until Monday afternoon. It was obvious he had been to work as he had his work clothes on. *Where had he been all weekend?* They weren't happy, outfoxed by a fox, the cunning bastard.

Chapter Twenty-Six

What a great weekend, thought Stranger as he drove to work that morning. *God I've been fantasising about this type of weekend for years and it all came true Friday night.* This nice-looking chick yelled out 'nice car' as I drove through Fortitude Valley. So, I stopped, and she came over and her next comment was, 'nice threads, nice car, good looking, you must be a nice guy'. All I had to say was 'jump in' and in she got, that easy, I could not believe it.

I asked her where she wanted to go and she said, "Anywhere with you."

She said, "I've just been released from prison and have nowhere to live."

I told her, "I've got a nice place and you can stay with me until you get on your feet."

I took her to my boss's house, a palatial home on acreage in Sheldon. I had the keys, as he lent me the keys years ago to pick up some gear/equipment from his house when I was first released on parole. I had made a copy way back then and had not had an opportunity or reason to use his premises. It's funny how fantasy turns into reality in a blink of an eye. As soon as I picked her up, a plan developed instantaneously. I knew he had gone away for a week; I'd have the place to myself. I must admit, I am looking better, the new clothes, supplements, gym work, and the last Botox shots make me look and feel ten years younger. Hell, she thought I was thirty-five. She was chatty, friendly, and was very affectionate as I drove her home to 'my place' for the weekend.

She told me, "My name is Michelle and I've had my parole cancelled for positive drug tests and have been released after serving my full term."

She looked about thirty-three but said, "I am forty-two and have two adult children who want nothing to do with me and neither do my family."

She added, "They all live in another State."

She was very impressed with the house, the bathroom, and the Jacuzzi. She made herself a drink from the bar. She liked bourbon and/or vodka and was delighted there was a supply of pot, some gear as well. She claimed that she never used drugs intravenously so was not positive for Hep C or any transmitted sexual diseases. After she had her first bourbon and coke, she had a line of speed. I pretended I was joining in, poured myself a coke, and when she came back from the bathroom I was sniffing as if I'd had a line of speed. We stayed up all night partying, and after a few hours of sleep, I took her shopping to buy some new clothes. All she wanted was new brand name sports clothes. We bought some supplies as she wanted to cook a good meal for me as she was impressed by the state of the kitchen that was full of gadgets. I paid cash for everything.

We returned home at noon, and after a luxurious bath in the Jacuzzi, she cooked a lovely meal of steak, mushrooms, and salad, followed by strawberries and ice-cream. She'd bought a few punnets of strawberries and the rest of them were made into strawberry daiquiris, followed by her favourite drink, black Russians. We had sex on and off all afternoon, between drinks and lines of speed. She was that out of it, she did not realise I was not. She was up for anything I suggested, a bit of bondage, or role playing where she sat on my lap pretending to be a schoolgirl. By

Sunday, I was tired of the usual sex and continuous chatter and talked her into the choking game when climaxing.

I told her, "There is nothing like it to experience."

I'd been daydreaming and thinking about strangling someone, anyone, for weeks. In the end, it was an anti-climax; she turned blue, stopped breathing, and that was it. I expected a bit of resistance from a woman like her, just like Janet had resisted. God, I'll have to get a fresh supply of drugs and replace what she'd drunk, the glutton, and glutton for punishment.

I decided I would have to dispose of the body and knew of a good spot. It was a vacant block of land near a vacant house at Capalaba. The place I'd hung Shelley from the window. I'd driven past this spot on the way to several jobs and thought at the time what a good spot for dumping a body. In suburbia, not far from the industrial estate, and no one lived nearby.

I'd have to clean up the boss's house, replace all the booze, dump the clothing she was wearing in an industrial bin and her new clothes to the charity bin in front of St Vincent de Paul's at Capalaba. *Never been worn. God, I'm generous.* I'll drop her naked body off on the way to my next job and check the boss's house on the way home from work to make sure everything is looking ship-shape.

I backed the boss's Toyota Hilux dual cab Ute onto the rear of the block of land, dug a shallow grave, and covered the area with leaf litter.

Good job, so easy, the next one will be different as I will have a plan before I choose my next victim.

I thought about the old guy I met in prison that had been convicted of several murders where the bodies were never found. He was called the 'Cutty Sak' murderer. He hired young blokes to work on his yacht to go treasure hunting and they were never seen again. I had befriended him in prison as no one else was game enough to talk to him as he was scary. He even made me tetchy, but this did not stop me from discussing the disposal of bodies with him and I knew I would utilise his methods of disposal on my next victim.

Chapter Twenty-Seven

Hargreaves and Plummer were inundated with work. They had a good reputation for finding missing people and received more surveillance work from their contacts at Centrelink and Work Cover.

They had a meeting to discuss strategies, who was going to do what jobs, and when they would be available. The white board came in handy as they developed a plan of action. They decided to back off Stranger and Pierce for a while to enable them to complete the simpler tasks before spending more time on them. They'd let the police put pressure on Stranger and the Parole Office put pressure on Pierce.

Six new cases had arrived, three missing persons, one Centrelink fraudster, and two Work Cover investigations. Denise and Carol took the missing persons jobs whilst Jed, Rosslyn, and Richmond took the other investigations due to having to obtain evidence of malpractice or fraud.

They made up files with all the statistical and available information on all clients. The missing persons file related to two missing teenagers, one male and one female, and one adult female who was listed as missing by her daughter who lived interstate. They had all the relevant information from concerned families that included descriptions, photos, contact phone numbers, and a list of friends and associates.

The missing male was nineteen years old, unemployed, and living with his grandparents. He had been told to move out due to his abusive behaviour and ongoing drug and alcohol use. The family were concerned as they had not been able to contact him or find out where he was and knew he was incapable of looking after himself. A follower not a leader, he was easily led and not as streetwise as he liked to think. He had plenty of identifying tattoos and was known to attend nightclubs on the Gold Coast and associate with bikes who owned tattoo parlours. As Carol and Denise read the information supplied by the extended family, they concluded he was a budding psychopath with narcissistic tendencies that was demonstrated by his past behaviours towards the family, he had no empathy for others, a self-centred Peter Pan. Strewth, they'd have to go traipsing around the bars and tattoo parlours on the Gold Coast. Or if they're lucky, he'll answer his phone as he won't recognise the number.

The missing girl had lived with her grandmother in Brisbane since she was fifteen as her parents could not control her. She settled down until she was seventeen and then became involved in the drug scene in Brisbane and left home after a fight with her grandmother. No contact since she left and no known associates. She was an attractive-looking girl with a large dragon tattoo on her back. Carol and Denise thought, *what is with all these children being bought up by grandparents.* They both knew the answer as they had come into contact with parents in the past who were usually in the drug scene and had lost custody of their children.

The last file informed that the missing woman was a forty-two-year-old career criminal. She had a few tattoos, Japanese writing on her wrist and a tribal band around her left upper arm. The only photo was a decade old, and her daughter had not seen her for several years. She thought her mother had been in prison in Queensland and had been recently released but she had not heard from her. Carol was certain she could obtain her release date and a more recent photograph from Margo.

They contacted the Police Service and Parole Service to see if anyone knew anything about the missing persons. The teenagers had no record on the system, but Carol and Denise were told by Gold Coast police where the local nightclubs were and where their person of interest would most likely attend. Denise and Carol went clubbing on the Gold Coast. They attended a couple of nightclubs after midnight and hid in the shadows observing the clientele. They tried to dress trendy but knew they looked out of place; everyone was so young. They felt ancient and a couple of young blokes thought they were old dykes. By the time they reached the third nightclub, Denise was developing a headache and Carol was getting agitated with all the noise and racket around them. Then they spotted him at the bar. He was spending money freely, seemed to know a few people, and was ordering Jack Daniels straight. He didn't look old enough to drink and they wondered how he could afford what he was drinking on the unemployment benefit. Denise phoned his mobile, and when he answered, she knew she had the right person. They had a moment of uncertainty, what to do now. They decided on the direct approach and walked up to him when he was alone, introduced themselves, and asked him to contact his family as they were worried about his wellbeing. He laughed and told them he was doing all right and they could tell his 'caring' family to get stuffed. They let him talk. He claimed he had toxic grandparents who had treated him badly since he was three years old. He blabbed on about what a perfect, sensitive child he was and how he could no longer live with his grandparents. He now had good friends in the tattooing business that looked after him. Denise and Carol told him they'd tell his grandparents they had found him and that he wanted no contact and leave it at that. When they left, they felt like failures. They could see he was living beyond his means and possibly involved in the local drug scene. They decided to pass his information onto the local drug squad, who knew of him but thought he was not involved in anything heavy. There was nothing further to do so they went home totally knackered. They would tell his family that he was okay tomorrow.

Margo came through with possible associates of the missing girl and where they hung out in Wynnum. A few criminals liked having attractive young chicks around and were always well supplied with marijuana and alcohol. They usually went to pubs with live music. A few days later, on a Saturday afternoon and night, they traipsed out again and did a pub crawl around the live music scene. They dressed in black t-shirts and jeans with sturdy boots and went from venue to venue. Some of the bands were quite good and at least they enjoyed themselves. They sat on their beers and had almost given up looking for the girl when Carol went to the toilet. In the ladies, she saw a girl with a skimpy top and short skirt who had a large dragon tattoo on her back.

She said, "Hi, good band."

The girl hardly acknowledged her and left to go back outside.

As Carol got out of the ladies, she saw that Denise had approached the girl and told her, "We've been looking for you as your grandmother wants to know where you've been and if you are okay."

Denise noticed she was hanging with known criminals and told her to contact home.

The girl said, "I'll contact Grandma."

And walked off. The blokes at the table she returned to

recognised Denise as she'd worked at the local court for many years. The next day, the grandmother contacted Hargreaves and Plummer to thank them. Her granddaughter had returned home. She told her grandmother that the guys she was hanging around with told her to go as they did not want any trouble. Denise and Carol had a good laugh about that, crims don't like trouble and they probably thought rightly that Denise would and could cause them some grief over this girl.

They had the latest photo of the missing mother. Michelle Farmer had been released from prison a week ago. She was supposed to go to a half-way house but did not turn up. They had no further information and told the daughter they would continue to check any leads they got but, at this stage, they were not hopeful.

Chapter Twenty-Eight

Jed and Rosslyn decided to do the Work Cover surveillance first and left Richmond at home with Carol. The job seemed straight forward. All that was required was to obtain photos and film footage of the two subjects regarding their daily activities. There was no question about their injuries but in their capacities or capacity for work.

They followed the first client, a forty-five-year-old cook, who received a back injury at work when a freezer door fell on top of her. They followed her around for a few weeks. She went to doctor's and physiotherapy appointments and walked to the shops every other day. They observed her carrying groceries some days and then did not see her for a few days as she never left her house. After they had obtained footage of her shopping, they noticed she now took a shopping trolley to the shops. She was a real chatterbox and seemed to like to talk to people. Rosslyn thought she would be able to bump into her at the shops and have a chat. Rosslyn started up a conversation at the chemist where her target was getting prescriptions filled. She told her of her back pain and injury at work and that she was on New Start Allowance, waiting on a compensation pay-out for her back injury. She said she was tired of taking pain medication as she did not want to become dependent on them. She now realised she would have pain all the time and had decided to manage her pain with exercises the physio had given her and would not do anything to aggravate her back. She told Rosslyn that when she was in a lot of pain, she would virtually be bed ridden for a few days if she overdid it. She claimed she could not return to work cooking due to the heavy lifting and was doing voluntary work at the local charity shop as part of her job capacity requirement. She said she enjoyed doing this as she liked clothes and believed she had good taste and liked talking to others. When Rosslyn got back to the car with her audio tapes. Jed had wondered why she had taken so long in the chemist.

Rosslyn laughed and said, "The target was indeed a real chatterbox."

They felt they had enough evidence to write a report and set off to check out the other Work Cover job.

The next two jobs were the result of relationship breakdowns, with both sides dobbing each other in to the relevant agencies. The next Work Cover job related to a thirty-eight-year-old male who had deliberately injured his foot with a high-pressure hose and claimed he was unable to work. They followed him for a few weeks and, at first, he did not appear to be doing any paid employment; he spent his time fishing or drinking beer. One day, he went and picked up a front-end loader and did some excavating work on a local property. The guy he did the work for appeared to pay him after he completed the job. They'd taken Richmond on this job and after the excavator left, Rosslyn bowled in after her naughty dog, who was digging up the upturned ground. She started chatting to the guy, saying she had just moved into the area and was thinking of hiring an excavator to do the overgrown yard but did not know who to get. He gave her the details of the guy he hired, said he was cheap and only did cash jobs and usually charged five hundred dollars. Rosslyn was noting all this information and noticed that Richmond was getting carried away with his digging. They went over to see what he was digging up and it appeared the excavator had disturbed what appeared to be a grave site as they could see part of a human arm. They were shocked and decided to call the Police. The guy told Rosslyn that he had owned the land and the vacant house next door for years and was about to knock down the house and build some units. By the time they left, it looked like a crime scene as the forensic unit and police had cordoned off the property. Rosslyn and Jed had all the information they needed for Work Cover and would discuss their findings with their contact there as to whether they should take the investigation further. They were going to propose to their contact that they would hire the target and obtain footage of the transaction.

The contact at Work Cover wanted Hargreaves and Plummer to hire the excavator and take footage of the work done and payment as this may also be a Centrelink fraudster. Work Cover was only looking at the capacity for work and the level of compensation to be paid. The Work Cover contact advised Denise that they had thought he had deliberately injured his foot at work but could not prove it. The next day, Jed hired the target to do a goldfish pond and level a bit of ground in his backyard. He taped the phone call and Rosslyn captured the whole job, including payment, on film. They now felt the Work Cover jobs were completed and submitted their reports, including audio tapes and film footage to support their report.

The Centrelink job was in relation to an ex-partner phoning to advise that her ex-partner, who was receiving a Disability Support Pension, was scamming them, making out he had anxiety/depression and was unable to work full time. As they watched him, he appeared to be a jovial character, he laughed a lot when he was talking to his friends. His life was fairly predictable; he attended his doctor's and psychologist's appointments on most occasions. He had no drivers licence as he was suspended due to his bad driving record. His record included several drunk driving and speeding offences, which in Carol's mind demonstrated an anti-social attitude. Rosslyn followed him around; sometimes he'd catch a bus and reach his destination. . At other times, he would appear agitated and either not get on the bus or would get off the bus a few stops later. Rosslyn had read up on panic attacks and thought this is what they look like in person. She observed bizarre behaviour in the shops, where he would be standing at the end of an aisle unable to move and then fleeing the shop without buying anything. Rosslyn obtained her footage and submitted her report to Centrelink, concluding that they would have to obtain a medical report on his mental state as, from her observations, the target was indeed suffering from some mental disorder and subsequent panic attacks.

Jed and Rosslyn were pleased with their work and surveillance methods but thought to themselves that nothing is that simple. They could hardly wait for the next Hargreaves and Plummer meeting so they could discuss the results of their surveillance with Carol and Denise. They knew those two had their finger on the pulse, so to speak, and would find out any further information from their contacts within the Justice System about the body found at Capalaba.

Chapter Twenty-Nine

The day started out overcast and by lunch time the rain had set in, so Stranger decided to call it quits and go home. As he was driving, he thought about how often he had been pulled over and checked by police during the last month. Hell, he had complained to his solicitor who advised him that he had no grounds to complain about harassment as he was pulled over for random checks as part of a public safety campaign. Even though he had not been charged or found to be doing anything illegal, he had the feeling that there was a vendetta against him. As he drove along, he wondered who was behind it. He could think of no one in particular, with the exception of the police themselves. As his thoughts drifted to what he had got away with and where the bodies were buried, he thought about how the Cutty Sak murderer had disposed of his victims that were never found. He started to daydream about his next victim and the disposal of the body. When he looked up, he realised he was travelling towards the dump site at Capalaba and nearly rear ended the car in front of him. It was then he noticed the police presence on the vacant land where he had dumped Michelle. Crikey, they'd found the body so soon. God, it was just over three weeks, and he had driven this route on a regular basis, he did not think she would be discovered so soon as no one had used this land for years. The traffic was building up as people slowed down to rubberneck the activity of the police. He tried to drive through looking unperturbed but began to feel agitated and stressed as he approached a copper who was directing traffic. She gave him an imperceptible look and acknowledgement as she directed him through the intersection. He started to feel the fear-flight response psychologically and was sure this copper pulled him over for a random check last week. He thought he recognised her; she had let him know she recognised him. He began to feel uncertain about his plans. Since he got rid of 'the body', he had taken three more prostitutes from Fortitude Valley and disposed of them in Moreton Bay, Cutty Sak style. That is cut up and weighed down for the sharks to eat. His mind drifted back to his past, where he'd disposed of his child victims in the scrub, in the middle of nowhere, where no one would find them.

He started to fantasise about how to kill his next victim. He was bored with his usual modus operandi of sex, drugs, and strangulation. It was all over too fast to savour the occasion. He'd come up with an idea but was not sure whether it would work as well as he visualised when locked into his fantasy of life and death struggles. He decided to try it on his next insignificant victim.

When he arrived home, he phoned Katherine Pierce and invited her and her kids to Sea-World over the weekend. He had plans for her and her kids and was grooming them for his future fantasy and diabolical idea, which had been formulating in his imagination. He now admitted that she had been a major disappointment. She was unintelligent and slothful. He was disappointed that he'd spent his time and money on making himself more attractive for her as he'd originally thought she was the kind of woman he could have a serious relationship with.

She presented well to the outside world, but to his dismay, he found the reality of her life a total waste of time and space. She worked as a lap dancer, kept an untidy house and dealt in drugs. When he started to take her out, she invited him home to meet her children. Her daughter, Adrianne, aged six, was cute, her boy, Tom, aged four, was a demanding little brat that he would gladly strangle. She had made an effort to clean up her place before he arrived, but he had a third instinct about cleanliness and thought that, though the place was tidy, it was not clean. He did not like filth and discovered that the other rooms were filled with discarded rubbish, clean and dirty clothes mixed together, an absolute pig sty that he could not tolerate. As he thought about her, he wondered why he was spending good money on her and her kids and then realised he would kill them all and dispose of them where no one would ever find them. He became aroused at the thought and decided he'd pick up a few more prostitutes and practice his new method to see if it works. Then, at a later date, do Katherine Pierce and her kids the same way.

Katherine wondered why she had agreed to go to SeaWorld with Peter Stranger. He had taken her and the kids out a few times, and appeared attentive and kind, but she did not like the way he looked at her, it made her feel grubby and she suspected she may have misjudged him. Her friend, Autumn, had warned her and told her he was dangerous but, on the other hand, she felt she had him under control and liked the fact he took her and the kids on outings they all enjoyed.

She put her worries aside and began to ruminate about her current situation with her probation officer. The bitch had done a surprise home visit and saw the mull bowl and bong and told her she was skating on thin ice and that she would apply to the court to have urine tests included on her Probation Order to monitor her use of illicit drugs. The bitch went on about the extra condition being a therapeutic condition rather than a breaching condition. What the hell did that mean? Katherine knew the answer to that one. She knew she'd have to cease her use of methamphetamine and marijuana. She was not pleased about the intervention and disruption to her lifestyle and income. She'd discuss her situation with Autumn when she saw her as she'd been around the system a few times and probably knew how to dodge and manipulate the urine test. She was not sure whether she could discuss Peter with her due to Autumn's warning as to how dangerous he was.

Chapter Thirty

Denise had suffered from night terrors for as long as she could remember. She woke up around two-thirty a.m. with a feeling of pending disaster. She got out of bed as she could not sleep and went into the kitchen to make a cup of tea. Her husband, Don, was sleeping as she left the bedroom. At four-thirty a.m. she received a phone call from her police contact who advised her they had identified the body at Capalaba as Michelle Farmer. Denise realised this was their missing woman from interstate. She contacted Carol at six a.m. who arrived at the office an hour later, accompanied by Rosslyn and Richmond.

They discussed the repercussions of this discovery. Carol had obtained the latest photo from Margo at the Probation and Parole Service. She now had the last photo taken of Michelle, which also included identifying tattoos. As they were looking at the photo, Rosslyn had a feeling, a deep sense that she had seen this woman before today. She could not for the life of her remember where she'd seen her, but the thought was disturbing her as she racked her brain for an answer. They decided to contact her daughter once her identification was confirmed by police and after the autopsy confirmed the cause of death.

As the morning progressed, Janet and Marcia phoned to make an appointment.

They spoke to Rosslyn and told her, "We want to see Carol and Denise urgently."

They had found out through their contacts in Fortitude

Valley that there were at least three prostitutes missing who had not been in contact or seen by their friends for several weeks. As she made an appointment, Rosslyn flashed on the image of the woman that had been seen with Stranger the night she and Jed had lost him in Fortitude Valley. She remembered the photo shot she had taken at the time and decided to enhance the shot to have a better look at it to see if she could identify this woman as Michelle Farmer.

Rosslyn started to get a nervous tummy and thought she may be onto something with the photo but then realised she had not had breakfast. She decided to order some food for their monthly meeting from Subway sandwich bar at Capalaba. The girls were coming in at two p.m. to meet with Denise and Carol. Jed arrived just before eleven a.m. in time for breakfast/lunch.

Denise and Carol made their reports to the meeting.

Denise stated, "I have been advised that several random road checks and random home visits have been conducted by police during the last month."

She advised, "No further evidence or incriminating material has been found but I have been told that Stranger had presented as verbally aggressive and antsy."

In summary, they thought they had aggravated him hopefully enough to make a mistake. On the other hand, he could become more careful. Carol confirmed that she had spoken to Kathryn Harrison, who indicated that Stranger was not happy with the ongoing surveillance and had considered making a complaint about being harassed. She had therefore advised him he had no grounds to complain as all checks appeared to be random. Kathryn was aware of the strategy to aggravate him but had kept this to herself when he had phoned for advice. Carol added that pressure had been put on Katherine Pierce by her probation officer in Brisbane. Carol knew that Pierce was not very happy with the extra scrutiny and the additional conditions that were added to her order.

She told the meeting, "Pierce now has to submit to random urine tests plus attend drug and alcohol counselling which will piss her off."

Jed could not advise of any further progress as he had been occupied with other work during the last month. He was getting fed up with following Stranger with no result.

Rosslyn was sorry he felt that way and told him, "I've been thinking about that time we lost him in Fortitude Valley. Remember when we were stopped by police for a random breath test? I took a photo of someone getting into Stranger's car."

Rosslyn had enhanced the images as much as possible, and with the extra details supplied by Probation and Parole, they studied the photos in earnest. Even though the images were blurred, the woman in the photo was about the same height and colouring of the missing woman. Jed and Rosslyn could just make out the tribal band on her upper left arm. They were now sure that the body at Capalaba was their missing woman, who appeared to be the last person to get into Stranger's car. Jed became enthused again and had decided to watch him at night for as long as it took.

Janet and Marcia arrived on time and ate the leftovers from lunch. They appeared in good spirits and spent over an hour filling in Denise and Carol about the missing prostitutes from Fortitude Valley and the gossip around the traps, which included a bit of gossip about Katherine Pierce.

Chapter Thirty-One

Stranger woke up the next day feeling the buzz and excitement of yesterday's discovery at Capalaba. The missing woman had been identified and police would not be releasing her name until they had contacted her family, who were interstate. The news report identified the victim's tattoos and requested any further information to be reported to police. They were looking for witnesses as they believed she went missing a few weeks ago and was last seen in Fortitude Valley.

He knew he had made a few mistakes when he dumped the body and clothes but felt confident that he would not be caught. He thought, smugly, that he had improved his method in murder as there were no other reports of missing women in the media. He no longer dumped bodies on the mainland. He dropped them in Moreton Bay where the bull sharks would dispose of and eat all the evidence. He let them go in little pieces, weighed down with heavy blocks of concrete. He was sure they would not be found, and if they were found, they would be difficult to identify. He kept his trophies at a location he had worked out a few years before for future hideaways. He was collecting gold chains, lockets, and bracelets that would continue to remind him of his escapades. He knew this was potentially dangerous but, in his psyche, he could not help himself. He utilised information he had obtained from the Cutty Sak murderer and was certain he would prevail and not get caught. He'd strangled a few, as per his old true and tried method, and experimented with the last two victims as he was getting bored with the sex and strangulation method. The last victim was the most satisfying. He had kept her alive and cut her throat; putting a plastic bag over her head. She watched herself slowly die as the bag filled up with her own blood. The expression on her face was priceless. The look on her face was one of shock and horror. Every time he thought of it, he became sexually excited and motivated to cause more havoc. He chose women who would not be missed by their families. He thought about his next victim and realised he would have to be careful as the news report indicated that the Capalaba victim was last seen in Fortitude Valley. He would have to find a new hunting ground.

He thought about Katherine Pierce and her children. He decided to continue grooming her and the children. He was getting tired of Katherine's untidiness and whinging, he was going to hang in there as he really wanted to dominate and groom her six-year-old daughter, Adrianne.

Chapter Thirty-Two

Spring had started with a vengeance. Jed, Carol, and Richmond had been watching Stranger for months. Carol had been away from Queensland for a few years and had forgotten how bad the midges and mosquitoes were near to the coast or near waterways, such as rivers, that had mangroves and mud flats. They were all itchy and even though they applied tropical strength repellent, it only seemed effective for a couple of hours. The warning on the bottle was to apply every six hours and Carol told Jed she'd heard of a fisherman in Northern Queensland who became very ill from not heeding the warning. They could not burn mosquito coils due to the smell and had to suffer in silence even though they were being eaten alive. They had been hiding in the bushes near the house from dusk until dawn where there had been some relief during the night. The damage had been done; they had welts all over them.

Stranger was on the move again. He came out of his house dressed up and spent an inordinate amount of time looking around his yard before he got into his car. This gave them the creeps. Following this guy was not for the faint-hearted. As soon as he left, they leapt into action and by the time they reached their car he was out of sight. By the time they reached the corner, they saw him turn left towards Brisbane. He was in no hurry, and as always, obeyed the traffic rules. He was heading towards the airport and for one awful moment they thought he was catching a flight to somewhere even though he'd have to have prior permission from ANCOR. They followed and watched him from a distance, parked several spaces away, and had to leave Richmond in the car. He casually walked to the departure and arrivals lounge where he sat down checking his watch and the arrival board. He was waiting for someone. The new arrivals on a flight from Los Angeles began to pick up their luggage and disperse. A beautiful young woman appeared and, after picking up her rather large suitcase, started 'looking around'. He approached her and started talking to her. He looked awkward as he appeared to be explaining something to her, and she on the other hand looked down at him curiously as he continued to talk. She was quite a bit taller than him and looked like Jennifer Hawkins with blond hair. Her most striking feature was her eyes. They were strikingly blue. However, her gaze was disconcerting. She appeared to focus on him with one eye as the other focussed on her peripheral vision. Otherwise, she was perfect. Stranger's chest puffed out like a bantam rooster as he accompanied her out of the airport. He carried her luggage and looked as proud as punch.

Carol and Jed waited a few minutes and left the airport. Jed was wondering who this woman was. Carol thought she knew but was not sure. Could she be his daughter? She remembered the photo he had shown her in an unguarded moment years ago, but as memories fade with time, she just was not certain.

They'd been following him for months and were uncertain of everything. He'd stopped going into Fortitude Valley at night and only attended the Criterion Hotel when Katherine Pierce was working. They went on picnics and fishing trips and presented as a happy family on happy family outings. Jed and Carol weren't prepared for the boat trips they took and, when it came down to it, had no idea what he was up to or indeed if he was doing anything at all. They had followed him to Carbrook, where he met Katherine Pierce and her children. He launched a boat loaded with crab pots, a large esky from a property that was situated on the Logan River. All they had to show for their efforts were welt marks all over their bodies. They were not happy campers.

Chapter Thirty-Three

Stranger drove straight home from the airport. They stayed up all night, talking, laughing, and catching up on the last twenty-five years. Holly told him her mother was doing well in the States and had returned to school and obtained a law degree. They both found this terribly amusing. He was enthralled by her appearance, confidence, and demeanour and for the first time in his life he felt the power of kin. A kindred spirit sat before him. He had got in some supplies of alcohol and drugs for this occasion. He'd bought five bottles of spirits and five bottles of liqueur as he did not want to appear as a straight arse or a cheapskate. Even though he knew he could not drink alcohol, he would tonight. He'd obtained some pot from Katherine Pierce, who was attempting to go straight and gave him her supply to get the shit out of her house.

They had a good night. She seemed pleased with his alcohol selection, and they drank a bottle of Wild Turkey and smoked a few joints. He was feeling loose and lucid and enjoyed her tales of Los Angeles and surrounds. It sounded like the last frontier of freedom as she told him about some of her tales of misadventure and near misses with the criminal justice system. They were both giggling like girls by the end of the night. They both had their own reasons and near misses, which to them made it funnier. However, both were guarded on specifics.

He decided to call in sick the next day. Hell, the way he felt, he could go to the 'good doctor' at Capalaba and get a medical certificate to cover the whole week. He never took a sickie but knew he could get some time off with a bad back. He tumbled off to bed happily at four a.m. determined to have more time with his daughter. He felt proud of her and began to have grand ideas about the future. She'd indicated that she liked his taste in alcohol but was not enamoured with the home-grown pot. By the end of the night, it was Los Angeles this and Los Angeles that in terms of what types of drugs she was used to doing. She was into pills, uppers mainly, but her preferred drug was cocaine. Mexican marching powder, she called it. Fuck, she was a laugh, he liked her more because she could handle her alcohol, didn't turn or get nasty, may have had her wobbly boots on, but hell, she drank most of the bottle.

The next day, he phoned in sick and told his boss he was going to the doctor. His boss sounded sympathetic and concerned when he told him he had injured his back at work on Friday. After he hung up, he had the feeling of moral superiority and righteousness. Now he knew where Donald Trump was coming from. What's it called? Righteous indignation? At that thought, he started to giggle as he made an appointment with the good doctor for two p.m. the next day. He'd practice his 'I've got a bad back' walk, take a walking stick, and get some pills. Janet had told him getting pills from the 'good doctor' was no trouble. Stranger liked Janet, she was a good sport, had lots of contacts, and he was sure she could get some pills, ecstasy, coke, and high-grade hydroponic pot or hashish. Only the best shit for his girl.

Holly walked in and wanted to know what was for breakfast and wanted to know what he was laughing at. He was glad he had stocked up his cupboards and she went for the big breakfast, eggs, bacon, tomatoes, and mushrooms on Turkish bread. He laughed again at her breakfast order and told her he was laughing because he had a good night and loved her company. She seemed pleased. He told her he was having the week off work and would show her around town and introduce her to his friends. That would be the hard part as he had few friends. In fact, he was a loner. The only people he saw were Katherine Pierce and her kids. His only friend would be Janet, who would be able to score for him and would introduce him as a friend to her large network of associates. When he thought about his lack of friends, he decided to contact a few parolees and criminals he had met in prison to expand his network. He knew they did not like him but also knew they would not turn him away. It was an unwritten code, the state of anomie where straight arses barely got a look in.

She'd told him she had a working visa for twelve months. He was glad she had the brains not to apply for a family re-union visa as he was the only family here in Australia. Christ, that would have gone down well, 'I'd like to apply for a visa to visit my father, convicted murderer, paedophile, and registered sex offender'. Fuck, he'd have to tell her, but not this week, way too soon. He wanted to show her off and have some fun, he'd like to relive last night over and over again.

He phoned Janet and another criminal he had met at Wolston Prison. He arranged to meet her for lunch the next day and the mate the day after. He never discussed anything on the phone, liked to do business in person even though he'd have to pay for lunch and drinks. He wanted to present as a good old boy to his daughter. He wasn't even sure why but could hardly contain this feeling, his sense of pride and hubris, this feeling of joy. He asked himself would this excitement last, would life return to the mundane? He was not sure, but he was willing to take the risk.

Chapter Thirty-Four

He arrived at the Koala Tavern at Capalaba just before noon. Holly wanted to play the pokies before lunch and appeared keen to meet his friends. Janet was already there playing pokies when they arrived. After a short introduction, he gave Holly fifty dollars to lose while he and Janet had a chat. He bought the drinks and sat down at a corner table. He got straight to the point. Janet listened attentively and indicated that she may be able to put him in contact with someone who could help him score. No names were mentioned at this time. She told him she was not in a position to score at the moment as she was keeping a low profile as she still had outstanding matters before the court and did not want to jeopardise her freedom.

The Tavern had been renovated since the last time he had been there. The food, however, had not improved. The usual menu of cheap schnitzels or overpriced, over cooked steaks was on offer. Everything came with a sad or average salad and chips. He was not impressed but Holly did not seem to mind or complain. She and Janet appeared to get on well and were chatting and laughing during lunch. Janet left to make a few phone calls, and after she returned, she gave him a phone number and an address at Tingalpa and told him to contact Dianne, who would be able to assist him, indicated the prices, and left with a promise to catch up at a later date. She had to pick up her kids from school.

Stranger phoned Dianne and placed his order in the coded

language Janet had advised him to use and agreed to meet her at four p.m. He then took Holly shopping for some clothes that suited Queensland's climate. He asked what they'd been laughing about; Holly told him that Janet had told her about her shopping expeditions at A-Mart sports. She wanted to go there to buy her new clothes, sports attire, and found this very amusing. She like her father liked to stay in shape. After they bought a few tank tops, tights, track pants, and running shoes, he took her to the gym he attended on a weekly basis. She liked the set up and watched the beautiful bodies work out. He enrolled her for a year. They had an hour to kill so he showed her around and they did a light workout. She was very fit and could hold her own in any gym.

They arrived at Dianne's ten minutes earlier than arranged and waited down the road. The address was not what he expected. The house was brick and modest, understated, and was set back from the road on about five acres. Around the house, the yard was well kept, and the gardens well maintained. The surrounding yard, however, was littered with old shipping containers and there was an old caravan down the back that appeared to have someone living in it. Dianne arrived on time. She drove a black Hyundai Elantra and had three children in the car. She indicated he should wait outside as she settled the kids inside the house. After about ten minutes, she went to the caravan and got his order, and he paid the grand he owed. He'd bought two grams of cocaine and a bag of dope. She offered to weigh it up for him there and then. He told her he trusted her as she was highly recommended by Janet. He would weigh it up at home to be sure. She offered them a beer as she wanted them to stay a while to appear as visitors not customers. They then went inside to have their drink that turned out to be a few drinks before they departed.

Dianne was quite chubby, but Stranger could tell that under all her weight she had once been a very good sort. Holly agreed with this assumption. The only thing they felt uncomfortable with was the scrutiny of her kids, particularly the boy, who was about eight years old and clearly knew what was going on. They spent an hour at the house and left with the goodies and new clothes. On the way home, they stopped and bought a pizza for tea that night.

As soon as they got home, they had a few lines of coke, a few more drinks, and nibbled at the pizza. They laughed and talked into the night. They discovered they were more alike than they initially thought, and like most families, they had the same sense of humour. All in all, it had been a good day and he hoped they would have many more.

Chapter Thirty-Five

Jed and Carol arrived as Stranger and the girl drove in and went into his house. They were usually set up before he got home from work, but they were running late. They let them settle in before taking their usual position, which had clear vision of the kitchen and living area. As the night progressed on, the noise, chatter, and laughter grew louder, and Jed decided to move closer to the house to get a clearer view of the occupants. They appeared to be doing lines in the kitchen. As Jed got closer, Stranger turned and looked out the window. Christ, he's got a sixth sense. Jed ducked down and stayed still for at least five minutes. His heart was beating rapidly as he tried to calm himself down. The girl then came out of the house holding a drink and commenced smoking a joint on the patio. Stranger turned away from the window and joined her. They chatted and laughed but it was hard to hear what they were talking about as they talked softly and kept their voices low. Like a low hum, very hard to decipher. Jed was kicking himself as he had put the surveillance equipment inside the house. During the months of watching him, he had spent little time outside on the patio. Jed could not figure out who this girl was and what kind of relationship she had with Stranger. He treated her like a friend and did not appear to be making any moves on her. They stayed up all night again. This was not usual. Jed felt something had changed. He and Carol left at seven a.m. Stranger was not going to work again. As they drove away, they had a lot more questions than answers and their frustration levels were high. They had spent a lot of time with no result, nothing to report, with the exception of a bit of illegal drug use.

Stranger got up at ten a.m. and was pottering around the house when police arrived. He had always been careful and had stashed and buried the remaining coke and pot in the compost heap in the backyard. His ANCOR officer was there with a smirk on his face and demanded he submit to a drug test. This amused him. He was a master at subterfuge. He'd fooled a lot of people over the years. He would appear to be actively involved in drug and alcohol use but did not participate. He knew from experience that those involved rarely took any notice of others when they were out of it. This enhanced his reputation as a good old boy with them but he liked to be able to control and to stay in good shape so he could maintain control over others. His daughter was no exception to the rule. He supplied a urine sample, which was clean, and they found nothing in the house. The police left after turning the house over, they were not pleased. Neither was Holly, who was unceremoniously chucked out of bed when her room was searched. After they left, she had a lot of questions to why they were there or why he had been targeted. He told her everything, or almost everything. He told her about his past conviction and his serious violent offender and ANCOR registration. He minimised his responsibility and told her he was a victim of legislation. That he'd done a crime, done the time, and was now subject to ongoing harassment by police. He knew he sounded paranoid but added this was what social control was all about. He told her about his past but not the present or his future plans. He thought she would be upset about his antecedents. She was, however, fascinated and then told him of her escapades in Los Angeles and surrounds. She claimed to have murdered seven males after seducing, drugging, and carving them up. She reckoned she fed them to the sharks. They were fascinated and in a facinorous state of mind. He had met his kindred spirit.

He kept his two p.m. appointment with the good doctor. He obtained some scripts for Oxycodone, Endone, and a sick certificate for two weeks. He arrived home at three p.m. with the goodies. He'd dug up the stash before he left so Holly could get mellow. She was pleased to see him back and was dressed to go out. They'd go cruising together and decided to go to the Gold Coast to check out the scene down there. He explained it was a different scene to Brisbane, more touristy, more glamorous, and definitely more fresh meat.

They spent the rest of the day on the patio, discussing their past adventures, how they planned and chose their victims, and how they'd never been caught for any of them. They discussed the importance of being careful and to rely on their sixth sense. The sense that warned them of a dangerous situation that then enabled them to adjust their plans. They both felt superior in intelligence to most people and their favourite by-line started to become 'paranoia is a good thing' or 'I'm not paranoid, I'm careful'. They found these sayings amusing, kindred spirits or kin that tend to laugh at the same thing, even words unspoken.

They looked and felt pretty good by the time they left Brisbane. He dressed for the older woman she dressed for the younger bloke. Tonight would be a surveillance run of the clubs so they could better target their victims. Whilst it remained unsaid, they both knew their intentions, they were so alike.

Chapter Thirty-Six

Jed had phoned Denise at home after they'd left Stranger's house and told her what he'd observed at the kitchen window. She then phoned his ANCOR officer who arranged to conduct a random home visit the next day. They knew he was a cunning bastard, but if he was taking illicit powder, they would have to strike within a day or two. They did not need a warrant for a home visit, so the sooner the better. They couldn't believe his house and Stranger were as clean as a whistle. Jed came to doubt his observation skills. While he did not see the mirror they were using, he did observe them taking turns with a rolled up fifty-dollar note, heard the sniff, and observed their behaviour and demeanour. They both appeared to be coked off their heads and shared drinks and joints throughout the night.

The police had no idea of the identity of Stranger's visitor; they did not ask her for her details as they were too busy shoving and harassing Stranger. All they knew was what she'd told them, that she was a visitor. She kept her mouth shut.

The mood at Hargreaves and Plummer was almost toxic. They'd virtually stalked Stranger for months and were none the wiser. Their strategy of police harassment was not making the impact they had expected. They expected him to make a mistake and become careless. Their strategy seemed to have the opposite effect. He became harder to follow, more careful, therefore more unpredictable. He ceased going on nightly jaunts to Fortitude Valley, was rarely seen at the Criterion Hotel, and saw less of

Katherine Pierce. Jed and Carol had lost him twice at Carbrook when he gave them the slip in the semi-rural setting. All they saw was the back of his head as he launched a boat at night. He had a large esky on board, a couple of fishing rods, and a crab pot. They were almost eaten alive by mosquitoes and midges waiting for him to return. They had waited all night until noon the next day. He did not return.

Jed and Carol were watching the house, and when the targets left at eleven p.m., they followed them and ended up at the Gold Coast. Stranger and the girl went into a nightclub, stayed an hour, and went to another club. Jed and Carol were refused entry to the clubs and were told they were too old and were not suitably dressed. They were neatly dressed in casual wear with running shoes on their feet.

They'd called it a night at two a.m. They'd waited around and figured out they were not the sort of clientele that the clubs let in. Jed and Carol were reflecting on their failures in surveillance and trying to figure out their next step, they returned to the office the next day. When they arrived, Janet and Marcia were there wanting to see Denise and Carol. After Jed left, the girls saw Hargreaves and Plummer.

The girls wanted to know if Denise had any success in getting their soliciting charges dropped. Denise indicated it was a work in progress and that the prosecutor felt their matters would be withdrawn due to lack of evidence. Janet then told them of the lunch date with Stranger and how she'd met his daughter, Holly, at the Tavern. She did not, however, tell them her involvement in assisting them in scoring drugs from Dianne. She and Marcia wanted the charges dropped before they would hand over that sort of information. Janet had a fair bit to say about Katherine Pierce and Stranger. She reckoned he had lost interest in her and had not been to her place for over a month. They told them the news on the street was disturbing and as usual no one was doing a thing about it. Carol was used to the circular way Janet communicated. She asked them what they were going on about. Janet and Marcia raised their eyebrows and sighed. Christ, these two supposed professional private eyes were dense.

"It's about missing prostitutes and their dead friend," they said in unison.

"Who are they?" Carol asked the girls.

When it got down to it, the girls did not know. Their knowledge was not specific, all hearsay and gossip from the girls working the street in Fortitude Valley. The general consensus, however, was that the missing girls were from out of town or runaways. No one had missed them, and no one was looking for them.

After discussing the possibilities for an hour or so, Carol had a light bulb moment after she listened to Janet as she told them about Stranger's daughter and their lunch date at the Tavern and how they loosely arranged to get together again. Carol said nothing at this time. She wanted to run an idea she had before Denise and Jed. She knew it could be dangerous, knew there was no reason for success, but also knew they were treading water and getting nowhere as far as finding out what Stranger was getting up to at night. He'd given them the slip a few times now, which led to confusion of their purpose. They also had egg on their face, so to speak, after Denise had put her reputation on the line and called ANCOR after Jed's phone call the other night.

Jed came back at two p.m. with a peace offering from the bakery; he was very apologetic about his misinformation.

Denise tucked into a caramel tart and shrugged, "That's the way the cookie crumbles. Not to worry, we'll catch him in the net one day."

They had a laugh about their consolation prize and tucked in.

They discussed the ongoing surveillance. Carol reckoned they could watch his house dressed as slugs.

She indicated, "I am getting pissed off about getting bitten by all sorts of critters when sneaking about hiding in the bushes."

As far as she was concerned, it was bullshit. That's how Carol's diatribe commenced with 'this is bullshit'. She highlighted their failure to obtain any evidence of missing girls, their discomfort in the surveillance, the mossies, midges, leeches, and ticks. She had welts and marks all over her body.

And with the start of summer coming, Carol added, "I am not keen about wandering around swamps full of mulch, full of bities, and the usual violent electrical storms that would come."

Carol stated, "The tick bite on my jugular was the final straw."

The allergic reaction she had when she pulled the tick off, she itched all over, under her arms, chest, and groin, she thought she was going to die. She could not swallow and had a panic attack; she had to lie down for a few hours.

Denise could hardly contain herself, thinking empathy, my dear girl, walk a mile in my shoes, as she casually said, "That's a good old panic attack."

No sympathy here. She, who had the night terrors, could be calm as a cucumber and a smartarse at the same time. This was a talent. Carol reflected on empathy and understood that you really did not understand the other person's position unless you really lived the experience. She would keep that thought in mind for future reference.

After the meeting, they decided to change their strategy once again. Denise would ensure the charges were dropped against the girls. Jed would enlist someone he knew from the SAS to continue the surveillance. They would have the girls work undercover for them as they needed people close to the source of the investigation. They would wait a few days before enlisting the girls. They would have to discuss the finer details with them once they knew what that was going to be. It would be better if Stranger contacted them rather than have Janet make contact, which would be out of character. The girls, it was decided, would have more success in entering nightclubs. They at least looked the part, scrubbed up well, and would be able to keep in touch and contact with the target. Denise was unsure whether this was a good idea. Carol, on the other hand, knew them well and was encouraged by the firm's acceptance of the idea. They still had to convince Janet and Marcia. That could wait a few days as Carol did not want to act on impulse. She knew the girls would act on impulse, so wanted them clear of the charges before putting them undercover. She knew they'd go for it. They liked excitement and were good at being sneaky and would like the idea of being imbedded behind enemy lines.

Chapter Thirty-Seven

The girls went for it, like a rat up a drainpipe. It had been a long time since they had been clubbing, like the old days when they were in their prime. Janet sent her kids to their grandmother for a fortnight. Her mother did not mind as she rarely saw the kids these days. She would not be sure how to entertain them but had plans to take them to Southbank and the theme parks on the Gold Coast. They tended to behave better for their grandmother as she was the only family they knew in their short lives. She had no computer at her place and tended to spend more time with them, and listened when they told her about school and things they liked to do. She was more patient than their mother, who told them to shut up and go play a game on the computer. Janet used the computer as a built-in babysitter, she'd pass but she would never make mother of the year due to her self-centred disposition and nature.

Denise and Carol told the girls what they wanted them to do, they insisted that they not go alone, and they would have to stick together in every situation.

Denise had good news about their soliciting charges and told them, "The charges will be dropped due to a lack of evidence."

The girls were elated about the charges being dropped and began to make plans for what to wear on their night out. They decided to do a recce run or reconnaissance to the nightclubs on the Gold Coast to ensure that they could get in at their age. Moreover, they would wait for Stranger to contact Janet. They did not want to appear too keen or intrusive. They knew that criminals had a certain protocol and would become wary if someone or anyone became too friendly if that was not their usual behaviour.

They loved dressing up and practiced their dance moves before they went clubbing. They shopped on the Gold Coast and had their makeup and hair done at a fancy salon. They definitely looked the part and at least ten years younger than their confessed forty years. They went clubbing three nights in a row and had no trouble getting into any club on the strip in the Gold Coast precinct. They booked into a resort for a week and laughed a lot about the ridiculous clubbers they encountered. They checked out both sexes and were astounded by the amount of shots these kids consumed in the pursuit of a good time. They danced together or with anyone who asked them for a dance. They had some chemical enhancement before they went out at around eleven p.m. They wanted to keep themselves a little together and not write themselves off as they'd seen some of the young folk do by that time of night. They were wary about scoring on the Coast and bought from a trusted source, Dianne at Tingalpa. Christ, they didn't need to be nabbed by Gold Coast Police, who appeared to be everywhere. Boy, how things have changed, they lamented, coppers everywhere, not like the old days when one could smoke a joint anywhere and line up in the dunnies. Nowadays, you had to be discreet. Thus chemical enhancement and legal drugs were the way to go these days. Within three days, they could pick out the chemically enhanced who drank water all night and the rowdies that downed significant amounts of shots of alcohol. The girls drank Benedictine and Cointreau but paced themselves, so it improved their general feeling of wellbeing. They laughed about their practiced dance moves, reminiscing about the clubs they went to in their youth. They need not have bothered practicing as everyone on the dance floor seemed to just jump around to the techno music. Well as in Rome, they watched, learned, and listened and, to their astonishment, they had fun.

Stranger called Janet as they were about to leave the Gold Coast.

She told him, "I am with a mate, and we've been away and living it up on the Gold Coast for the last few days."

They agreed to meet the following night as he wanted to take Holly to some night spots on the Gold Coast. Janet and Marcia extended their stay at the resort. They agreed to meet at the resort.

Janet told him, "Our room number is 109, and you'll have to be here by nine thirty p.m. so we can have some canapés before hitting the clubs."

She knew he understood what she meant, words unspoken, an intuitive leap, or was she only surmising.

The girls bought another outfit and went to have a makeover at the resort's beauty parlour. By the time Stranger and his daughter arrived, both girls felt like partying. Janet introduced Marcia to them, explaining that she was her oldest friend; acceptance was what she was aiming for with the introduction.

They both looked gorgeous, and Stranger could not take his eyes off Marcia and remarked, "Why have you not introduced her to me before tonight?"

Janet was taken aback, she then hinted that she wanted to keep him to herself and didn't need any opposition. He seemed to accept this at face value, but he did indeed like the look and charm of her best friend.

Holly bought out the coke and they all had a few lines, even Stranger as he could not fake it before the two professionals. They went clubbing until dawn. Between clubs, they went back to the resort for more lines. Holly insisted on this so who were they to argue. By the end of the night, they had showed off their dancing prowess when the music they knew was playing and jumped around with the rest of the crowd when the techno music came back on. They all had a great time, even Stranger, who left at dawn with Holly. They agreed to go dancing again, the night after next, as the girls and Stranger cited old age and a need to rest. Holly, on the other hand, could and would have gone out night after night but agreed to their wishes. The girls decided to have a quiet day the next day and relax at the spa and pool at the resort.

Chapter Thirty-Eight

As Stranger and Holly drove back to Brisbane, they listened to the radio. Paul Kelly's 'I've done all the dumb things' came on the radio. Holly had not heard it before and was happily singing the chorus; he looked over and thought she's pretty cute. He then reflected on the previous night. He'd certainly done some dumb things last night. He never touched illicit drugs. He did not know what had got into him; he was usually so controlled in social settings. Was it the enthusiasm of the girls or was it the vicissitude of the company he was keeping? Holly and the girls were on the same plane all night. They had a connection with Holly, the words unspoken type that he thought he had with his daughter, but this was different, it was a female thing. This occurred to him when they were perving on and checking out the young things at the bar. He'd have to talk to them later about this, he thought he understood but was not exactly sure.

He had to know if his schemes were going to work. He then thought of the coppers. Christ, he'd be gone if they pulled another random check on him. He then suggested to Holly that they book into the resort at the Gold Coast for a few days. It would give him time to straighten up and get the drugs out of his system. They decided they would go home now, pick up some clothes, booze, and more coke and return to the Gold Coast that day.

Janet and Marcia spent the morning dozing off and cool towelling it. They spent some time in the spa and had a massage. They intended on having a quiet night, an early tea, and a good night's sleep. They really let their hair down last night and were paying for it.

"Not as young as we used to be," they both said and reflected that it was, "Hard keeping up with the youthful Holly."

They both thought she was all right.

Janet reckoned, "She can handle her drugs and alcohol, has a wicked sense of humour, and a perverse idea of what is funny or amusing."

In particular, checking out the fresh meat at the bar, looking at the little people trying to be big shots. That's what they were laughing at, 'the rebels without a clue who were posers and dickheads'. They had no idea Holly was thinking about victims of her perverseness.

They were surprised when Stranger and Holly rocked up later that afternoon. They had told them they would be having a night in as they'd been partying for the last three nights. They had agreed to meet the next night and were genuine when they said they'd be looking forward to it.

By the time Stranger and Holly booked into their room, they had ordered some food and drinks and were prepared to stay in for the night. Holly indicated she may check out one of the clubs they'd been to the previous night later in the evening. Stranger went to bed. Holly went out later that night. She'd seen the perfect victim the night before but did not have an opportunity to chat him up. He was the one the girls found amusing, they'd thought he was a bit of a poser and a dickhead. Holly could see what he really was, aside from the tattoos and his gentle manner, she saw him as a lonely boy with very few real friends. She was determined to meet, seduce, and murder him in that order. She went out later that night, but he was not there. She asked the barman whether he would be in later. He did not know as he had just started his shift. He did, however, know who she was talking about and reckoned he'd be in again tomorrow night. That decided it for her; she had a shot of Drambuie and went back to the resort to have a good night's sleep.

Chapter Thirty-Nine

The girls had a good night's rest and were relaxed and energised. By lunchtime, they met up with Stranger and Holly again after they'd returned from picking up extra clothes and drugs from Brisbane. The girls and Holly picked up from where they left off two nights ago. They had a few lines of coke and dressed up for another night on the town. Stranger had one bourbon and declined a line of coke, saying he was not feeling too well and thought it best not to indulge tonight. They did not seem to mind and by the time they left the resort they were ready to party.

It was decided that Marcia would stay in control so they would have a better idea of what happened during the course of the evening. She figured a few lines of coke would not impede her observation skills. No alcohol tonight, she'd decided, or better still a few drinks but would not try to keep up with Janet and Holly. God, those two could party, they were competitive, and Marcia observed that they appeared to be drinking shots from the top shelf, dancing, chatting up young blokes, and ducking off to the toilet every hour or so. Everyone appeared energetic and danced like there was no tomorrow. Marcia was cruising and thought everyone there was out of their heads, all except Stranger, who was very subdued and looking a bit flat. Marcia knew from experience that conversing with him would irritate, so they sat in their booth in silence, observing the night's entertainment. She also reckoned the staff were chemically enhanced and were on very friendly terms with the patrons. By one a.m. the place was rocking, and she noticed Holly at the bar chatting up 'lonely boy'. Janet was nowhere to be seen.

An hour later. Janet re-appeared and told Marcia, "I've been in the VIP section of the club and had lines off the table."

She was blathering on about something when Marcia noticed Holly leaving with 'lonely boy'. Stranger noticed this as well but stayed where he was and offered to buy her a drink. She accepted the drink and chatted to Stranger about how things had not changed a lot in the clubbing scene over the years. They felt like aging perverts when they looked around the room at all the young things. Marcia thought she may have spoken out of turn, but Stranger laughed, and they both laughed out loud. They both knew their own backgrounds, from prostitution to perverts. They drank to that and decided that, after they finished their drinks, it was time to leave.

Then the night turned to shit in minutes. People scattered everywhere and everyone dropped their drugs on the dance floor.

"Christ, it's a police raid."

Stranger and Marcia looked at each other and muttered, "Fucking Gold Coast Cops."

They remained calm as they were probably more together than most of the patrons. They had an anxious moment when police searched them and then let them go. The police were more interested in checking the staff and the VIP room and rounded up all the usual suspects. When they got outside, they bumped into Janet, who had ducked out for a cigarette before the police arrived. Stranger was glad Holly had left earlier as he knew she had some coke on her. He was relieved after Janet told him she would have been cool as they'd used all they had on them by one a.m. They went back to the resort to the girls' room and chatted until dawn. Marcia was starting to think that Stranger was all right.

Stranger got back to the room he was sharing with Holly at dawn. All was quiet. He went to bed to have a few hours' sleep. When he awoke, he got quite a shock as Holly was sitting on the end of his bed.

Before he could say anything, Holly told him, "I've stuffed up and we have a problem."

He was dazed from lack of sleep as she led him into the adjoining room. There lay 'lonely boy', dead as a doornail on the floor.

Holly made no excuses and shrugged her shoulders and muttered, "Shit happens."

Stranger thought the same. No use crying over spilt milk.

He told Holly, "Put the 'do not disturb sign' on the door and sit tight."

He went to his Ford Territory and came back with a tarp and some ropes. He then expertly rolled up and wrapped the body in a neat bundle. He decided there and then not to put the body in his vehicle but would go back to Brisbane to pick up Jack's boat. He told Holly to hang about and that he'd be back in two hours.

When Stranger got back to Brisbane, he had contacted his old mate, Jack Donnelly, now a retired criminal who was, in his time, the best fence in the business. Jack lived at Capalaba in an old fibro house that was situated on a large block of land. Jack had done well and needed the space for his toys that he was now too old to use.

Stranger told Jack, "I want to hire your boat again so I can take Holly and some girlfriends out fishing."

That was, of course, if they would come for an outing and reconnaissance for further dumping sites. Jack was pleased to see him and would not hear about any payment for the hire of the boat, all he wanted was that he put fuel in it and take it for a good run.

Stranger took the boat and arranged to see him again the next week and told Jack, "I will need it for a few days, like last time, depending on the weather."

It was a good boat, slept four, and Jack had told him, "The engine is new and it has been recently serviced but it does need to be used as boat engines seize up if not used regularly."

By the time he returned to the Gold Coast, Holly was excited about going clubbing again and knew her father would fix the problem from last night's efforts. They had enough cocaine to see them through the night. Holly seemed to need extra stimulation and the company of the girls as she appeared easily bored and he did not want that to happen.

True to his word, he was back in two hours with the boat and put the body in the front of the boat in the sleeping section. He'd filled the esky with soft drinks, bait, and snacks. He had fishing rods and hand lines on board. He intended asking the girls out on the boat but would have to first get rid of the package. He knew where he was going to unload it as he had surveyed the waterways between the Gold Coast and Brisbane and thought he knew the perfect place on South Stradbroke Island. There were numerous fishing shacks that were used by generations of fishermen. Some were still used by their families, but some were abandoned and left to neglect by disinterested families. He knew of one such shack and had used it in the past year.

He went to ask the girls, "Would you like to go fishing later today? I am a good captain, have a boat licence, and have borrowed the boat from a friend."

He said, "I am taking it out for a run with Holly and will be back in two hours."

It was such a beautiful day the girls did not hesitate after they checked out the boat.

They said, "Yes, we'd love to go."

Stranger and Holly launched the boat at Labrador without any problems.

Stranger was pleased with the boat and the promised company later on that day. It took about ten minutes to arrive at the hut. He moored the boat and waded ashore with Holly. He had a key to the padlock, which was new as he had recently been there to clean up the place after he disposed of his last victim. As far as Holly could tell, this place had all you would need. A camp stretcher with a mattress, solar power, gas camping stove, gas bottle, lights, and a camping table with two chairs. The view was magnificent, and the hut was spotless. Holly sat on one of the chairs, admiring the view and soaking up the atmosphere and the sun.

Stranger removed the bundle and dumped it unceremoniously in the middle of the room. Because he had been there before, he was well equipped with a battery operated chainsaw. He dismembered the body into smallish pieces. After he wrapped, tied, and attached the weights to the tarp, he tossed the package into a large tub at the back of the hut.

He told Holly, "We'll be back later to pick up the burly."

And laughed as he had mixed the parts up with rotting fish parts.

They left and returned to Labrador to pick up the girls. They were going on a fishing expedition later that night as he always found it was best to do these things after dark. He was sure the girls would not be keen fishermen and would only enjoy the boat ride in daylight hours. He'd phoned them and they met him at the boat ramp. He was right; they had worn their swimmers and had packed a picnic lunch. He would have to return later on with Holly to clean up the hut and dump the bucket of burly.

Chapter Forty

After a rough start to the day, things improved dramatically by the afternoon. They picked up Janet and Marcia at Labrador and proceeded down the waterways, past South Stradbroke, all the way to Russell Island, which is parallel to North Stradbroke Island. They'd completed a very scenic tour around the Moreton Bay Islands to the mouth of the Logan River. Stranger did a commentary on the places they had been, commenting on the fishing shacks on South Stradbroke, Jacobs Wells, and the mouth of the Logan River. The commentary was mostly a history lesson of the islands, the nature of the currents and deep shelves that one could allegedly conceal dumped bodies.

The girls were impressed with his local knowledge of the area. They'd stopped a few times to drop in a line and place crab pots to check on the way back. They'd caught a few bream and flathead and stopped at a beach on the south end of Russell Island and had a picnic lunch at the Lions Park. Not a bad spot, it had barbeques and toilets and you could see the Gold Coast. They both exclaimed how beautiful this part of the world was as they had lived in Brisbane for the last twenty years and had never been boating and did not realise how close these areas were to each other by the waterways. It was a beautiful day, the water was calm, and the picnic lunch was top notch. The girls had surpassed themselves as caterers of fine food and wine. They drank good Australian wines accompanied with a platter of olives, cheeses, dips, and in-season fruits. They laughingly toasted multiculturalism. Stranger remained sober as he took his captain's role seriously and appeared to be a confident and competent boatman. This impressed both Marcia and Janet as they were initially apprehensive about going out in such a big boat, not knowing how well Stranger would drive it. They had in the past gone boating on the Gold Coast with an associate who was intent on scaring them by speeding and taking short cuts across sandbars that turned them off boating for life. To their surprise, they thoroughly enjoyed the day, had a lot of fun, caught some fish, and picked up a few mud crabs on the return trip. They did not go swimming as Stranger advised them the bay was full of bull sharks.

Stranger was impressed with the effort the girls had made to make this trip an astounding success. Holly appeared to be enjoying herself and her mood seemed elevated, considering the gruesome start to the day. On the way back to Labrador, as they passed the fishing shacks, Holly commented on how they had forgotten the burly. Stranger shot her a look that could kill, and she abruptly changed the subject and started blathering on about the wonderful day they were having and how beautiful the waterways were on the Gold Coast."

Janet and Holly were getting on like a house on fire and making plans for future fishing trips with the possibility of staying out all night. Marcia knew her friend was a bit like that, in that if she had a good time, she would want to continue the good times on other occasions. Marcia knew from experience that this was a human fault and that the following time or occasion rarely met the expectation of the participants. She was filing information away from the day, placing in her memory the locations and comments made by Stranger. She decided she would write all the details down when they returned to the resort as she felt Hargreaves and Plummer expected a full and lucid report on their return to Brisbane.

Later that night, or more correctly, early morning at two a.m., Stranger took the boat out alone. He'd given Holly and the girls enough money to go shopping and to have a nice dinner in Surfer's Paradise. He returned to the shack, packed the burly in the front of the boat, and proceeded to steam clean and bleach the premises. There was not too much blood to clean up as lonely boy had been dead for several hours and Stranger had done the carving of the meat over a plastic tarpaulin. He revisited several of the fishing spots and dropped the head and hand with the burly and left the rest of the remains weighed down at his favourite body dumping site near Russell Island. He arrived back at the resort at dawn and went straight to bed, leaving a note for Holly not to wake him up until later that day. He wanted and needed to talk to her about the previous night's escapade. He needed to know more about her antecedents. She seemed a lot like him, and he was considering telling her about his past escapades and what he was really into. He felt she would understand and indeed could become an asset for his nocturnal activities. He felt sure the girls had not noticed or indicated any interest in them other than being there and having a good time. But due to his nature, he could never be sure.

Chapter Forty-One

Jed had enlisted an old army comrade, who had been released or discharged due to suffering from post-traumatic stress disorder. His mate, Brian Taylor, 'Tatts' to his mates due to the body art all over his body, was reliable when sober but could become vicious and dangerous when he was drunk. He'd have to keep an eye on his drinking but knew that if he kept him busy and off the rum, which was usually a precursor to his violence, he would be an asset to the surveillance of Stranger's activities.

They had been waiting and hiding in the bushes near the house when Stranger and the girl returned. They observed them leave within the hour and saw that they had each packed a bag and they appeared to be going out again. Jed decided not to follow at this time as Carol had been in contact with Janet, who had told her that they planned to book into the resort where the girls were staying at the Gold Coast. Carol knew they were going clubbing but did not know about the chemical enhancement, only the purpose of the trip. Janet did not tell her about the drug use but told Carol they appeared to be casing the clubs, but they could not figure out what they were actually up to. She had promised Carol that she and Marcia would stay close and would keep themselves together as she explained the first night was a 'getting to know you' night and they'd all got drunk and therefore were not paying any attention. They'd been showing off a bit and having a laugh.

She told Carol, "We will keep it together during the next few days and will try to find out or figure out what these two are up to."

Jed and Brian decided to do a bit of breaking and entering before they left as they needed to retrieve the surveillance tapes that Jed had planted on his previous visit a month ago. It seemed longer than that, how time flies when you're having fun. They broke in, searched the house, and removed and replaced the tapes, which they knew could not be used in any prosecution as they were illegal. It was for their information only. Carol knew about the tapes but had not told Denise as she knew she would not approve but she also knew Denise would come around if only for further information and intelligence on Stranger.

Brian found a passport belonging to Holly Bell, now they knew her name, Stranger's daughter from Los Angeles. They'd known that detail from Janet but now they had a name. 'Hell's Bell's' they called her as they returned to the office. Denise and Carol would be pleased. They also knew they'd have to run it by Carol and check the tapes before informing Denise. They decided to let Carol tell Denise as they both did not want to face the opprobrium from Denise as they wanted and psychologically needed her respect.

When they got to Hargreaves and Plummer, the only ones there were Rosslyn and Richmond.

Rosslyn told them, "Denise and Carol are out on a job, and I am closing up for the night and going home."

They told her, "We have retrieved and replaced the tapes at Stranger's and have the identity of Stranger's daughter."

They insisted that they wanted to run it by Carol as they had broken into Stranger's place again.

Jed then introduced Brian to Rosslyn and said, "He is my new surveillance partner as Carol did not cope well with insect bites."

Rosslyn was pleased to meet Brian as she knew how and what Carol felt about lying in the bushes, knew she was a bit soft, a bit of a sook when it came to insects, ticks, leeches, midges, and mosquito bites. Richmond, on the other hand, appeared wary and looked like he was going to bite him.

Rosslyn saw this and told Brian, "Don't pat him," and told him, "Keep your hands in your pockets."

She indicated that Richmond had a tricky temperament, but underneath she knew it was possibly Brian that had a tricky temperament.

She'd discuss the new recruit with Jed in private and said, "I'll contact you tomorrow after Carol and Denise have been updated with the information on the tapes."

As they left, Rosslyn knew Carol would probably allow them to continue what they were doing as she was used to blurring the lines as long as the outcome was what they needed. She also knew that Carol would have to use her persuasive power to get Denise on board. No good yelling and screaming to persuade either of them. They both needed gentle persuasion or otherwise they could get really, really stubborn, even to the point of a destructive outcome.

Chapter Forty-Two

The next day, the girls went to see Holly to tell her they were going back to Brisbane.

Stranger was still asleep, and they told Holly, "We'll catch up with him later as we don't want to wake him up."

They went for coffee and Holly thanked them for coming to the Gold Coast and showing her a good time. She claimed she had a blast and was keen to catch up at a later date.

The girls checked out and returned home. Janet figured she still had ten days of freedom without her kids. Marcia, on the other hand, needed some time alone and some space to enable her to sort out her thoughts and emotions about the four days on the Coast. She was surprised that she liked Stranger as she had habitually disliked him because of his treatment of her friend. She also knew Janet could be a handful and could irritate people. She knew her friend was wilful and stubborn and would stop at nothing for a good time. On the other hand, she could be thoughtful and kind. She could definitely drive people to distraction. What were her feelings about Stranger and Holly? She reflected on the drug and alcohol-fuelled few days and though she felt fairly straight, her thoughts drifted to the last forty-eight hours. She was sitting in quiet contemplation. She had to smile, and she had to admit to enjoying their company and had not had such a good time for many years. She did, however, take her surveillance activities seriously and had kept a journal of the last four days. She noted times and places, how they chose venues, what they did, where they went, and any relevant details. She did minimise the level of substance use on the grounds that she was not about to incriminate herself or Janet.

Upon reflection, her journal read like a QP9, it is an arresting police officer's report. She had to laugh about that and knew she would have to contact Hargreaves and Plummer. She decided that tomorrow would be a better day as she did not feel up to it today. She had to admit to herself that she felt apprehensive and slightly sad. When she thought about their adventure, she felt butterflies and sick to the stomach.

Janet arrived at Marcia's house mid-afternoon with a six pack of Jim Bean bourbons.

She told Marcia, "I was at a loose end and did not know what to do at home."

No kids, ten more days of freedom, and she felt lost.

Marcia reminded her of their task and said, "We have ten whole days of discovery."

And she made it sound exciting. Janet reacted like the chameleon she was, and her mood changed as her spirit lifted. They decided to give Hargreaves and Plummer an update tomorrow and would wait a few days before contacting Stranger and his daughter. They arranged to attend the office at Capalaba the next day. And spent the rest of the afternoon organising their thoughts about their activities so they would be able to give a coherent account of the previous days and nights they had spent with their targets.

They arrived as arranged at two p.m. Everyone was there to listen to their report. Janet was amazed at the detail of her friend's report. God, she was good and gave a lucid and clear account of all activities. The good old, how, what, when, and why report. She did not hold back and described the drug and alcohol use of all participants, indicating that they had to use some coke so as not to appear too straight. She described the nightclubs, who they chatted with, and gave a good account of the fishing trip, highlighting the points of interest.

Denise and Carol thanked the girls profusely for their efforts and told them to continue their surveillance. They all felt they had ten days to find enough evidence to enable the police to be involved.

After the girls left, Denise and Carol summarised the information that was gleaned from their surveillance work. They had times and dates, registration of the boat he utilised and allegedly borrowed from a mate. They also had a good description of the fishing huts on South Stradbroke Island and locations of interest around the Moreton Bay Islands. Carol was very familiar with the waterways as she and Rosslyn had been keen fisherwomen in the past. The description of lonely boy reverberated in their memory. Carol and Denise simultaneously came to the same conclusion. It was one of their missing teenagers. Denise and Carol considered passing the information to Queensland Police but still thought they needed further evidence.

Rosslyn was manning reception whilst the meeting was in progress.

She received a call from a previous client, who told her, "My grandson has not been in contact with me and appears to be missing. Rosslyn knew that he had told Denise that they could get stuffed but passed the message on to Denise anyway."

Upon receiving this information, Denise contacted Gold Coast Police and told her contact about their investigations and that the boy was now missing. She hoped she was not too late as she wanted and requested her contact to try and get the tapes from the club, fearing it may be too late.

To her surprise, her contact told her, "We have the security tapes from the nightclub concerned as we conducted a raid and they were confiscated as evidence for future prosecutions."

Denise gave all the information she had to her contact and felt they had made significant progress since enlisting the girls in their investigation. They all decided to continue watching Stranger. Jed and Brian would do the nightshift while Denise and Carol would conduct surveillance during the day and would treat it like a Work Cover investigation.

They prioritised their list of actions to be completed before their next meeting. The next stage of their investigation would commence tonight. They still had to listen to the tapes from the house, would check out the registration of the boat. and would go to the Gold Coast to check the security tapes from the nightclub.

Chapter Forty-Three

On their return to Brisbane, Stranger asked Holly, "What happened at the Resort last night."

She shrugged and said it was an 'unintended consequence'. Unintended as she did intend to murder him but not that night.

She explained her actions. "It was a consequence of lonely boy's irritating behaviour and the way he behaved when he was having sex with me."

She claimed he changed from a sweet, shy victim to a pervert that thought he was Casanova.

"In other words, he treated me like a whore," she told her father. "I just lost it and strangled him with his own belt in a sex game."

Fair enough, thought Stranger, and he told Holly about the woman he picked up in Fortitude Valley a few months before. He thought that incident was probably an unintended consequence as she had irritated him with her neediness and stupidity.

The diatribe all the way back to Brisbane was about 'things that shit me'. Christ, they were similar in mind and soul. They told each other of their past exploits and laughed at themselves all the way home. It almost or did become 'anything you can do I can do better'. They decided then and there to team up and double the fun.

Stranger told her, "I almost slipped up when disposing of my last victim's body, the one I picked up in Fortitude Valley."

He assured her, "I have now perfected the disposal of bodies, but I continue to keep a souvenir or memento from each victim."

She admitted, "I took lonely boy's nose ring."

And showed it to him.

He told her, "I will stash it in a safe place, where I keep my own stuff."

He would not tell her where his safe place was, but they could retrieve any mementos when they wanted, when they felt like reliving the moment.

The discussion then turned to hunting grounds and victims. As far as they were concerned, you were one or you were not. They discussed the virtues of reconnaissance, to check out areas for potential victims carefully before deciding on the victim. They had been careless and knew they had to lift their game.

When they arrived home, Stranger parked the boat under the carport. They'd use it again.

He placed a call to Jack to ask him if he could hire the boat again as he was showing his daughter around and that they'd had a terrific day on the water and had taken a run around the Gold Coast. He assured Jack that the boat went well, and they were considering going out again in a few days.

Jack insisted, "I don't want any monies for the hire of the boat, and I am glad someone is using it and keeping it running as boats deteriorate in driveways."

Stranger thanked him profusely and knew he would take Jack some fish or mud-crab in return for using his boat. *Quid pro quo* he thought to himself, *I may be a murderous bastard, but I know when to treat my friends right. Not that I have many friends, but the ones I consider my friends, I do the right thing by them.*

Holly was extraordinarily cheerful when they got home. She'd made a late lunch for both of them and was having a bourbon and coke.

She genuinely liked the girls and told Stranger, "I have discussed an overnight fishing trip with Janet, and she is keen to go."

She was like Janet in that she wanted to relive the good times again and again.

Stranger said, "I will ask them out on the boat for an overnight trip."

He knew Janet was a good sport from past experience, he also liked Marcia. She was different. To him, she appeared much quieter and thoughtful and respected other people's space and did not fill the conversation with banal comments. Janet and Holly were terrific fun, but they became tedious after a few hours. On the other hand, they were also very amusing. They tended to lack control. That's what he liked about Marcia; she had some control over her behaviour and only spoke when she had something to say. *Yes*, he thought, *I'll invite both of them out on the boat*. They could have a legitimate fishing trip as he and Holly trawled for another victim.

They discussed victims who became unaware of their surroundings and safety. Addicts were a good source; they were usually burned out and they looked like victims. The best victims were people with no connection to family; party girls and boys who had burnt their bridges with family and friends and were easily manipulated. They both loved reading true crime books to check modus operandi and were interested in how people were caught. They felt confident they would not fall into the same traps. Christ, who'd be silly enough to stuff bodies in freezers or fail to dispose of them properly. They knew keeping trinkets was dangerous but decided whatever they kept would be kept in plain view. As the discussion progressed, Stranger thought about Katherine Pierce and his first impression of her as a victim. He put the question to Holly, would she kill children? And she indicated that it would 'depend on the situation'. She considered this for a few minutes and sighed and said it would 'depend on the child'.

He told her about Katherine Pierce and said, "I met her several months ago at a club in Buranda called the Criterion Hotel where she works as a lap dancer."

He admitted, "I have not been in contact for a while but have considered seducing her and her kids but have been side-tracked with other activities."

He explained that he'd been turned off by the slothfulness and chaos of her house and had to have some time off. He still considered her a good victim, and thinking about her whole situation, she would not be missed by many. She definitely had no contact with her family or the father of her kids. The only regular contact she had with anyone was her probation officer in Brisbane. He thought he knew what their reaction would be if she failed to turn up for an appointment. Hell, they'd send a couple of letters, and if she continued to fail to attend appointments, they would conduct a home visit. If she was not there, they'd think she'd done a runner and would put out a warrant for her arrest. If her probation officer was really thorough, she or he would check with the Department of Families and or Centrelink. He was not really sure whether they would do this; he would have to discreetly ask the girls as they'd been through the system several times. He would have to contact the girls to arrange an overnight fishing trip for the following night, weather permitting, and if this trip suited them. He was thinking out loud and Holly seemed to agree, they would need more planning in considering if this victim and her family would be a suitable target.

Chapter Forty-Four

Hargreaves and Plummer felt they'd collected enough new evidence on Stranger and decided to call another meeting and invite the girls. They needed to focus their investigation and instead of operating on single points, they would call the team in and include input from Janet and Marcia. Rosslyn arranged the meeting for eleven a.m. the next day. They all agreed to attend, including Kathryn and Margo.

Jed and Brian arrived early, made their way to the meeting room and helped themselves to coffee and snacks. Due to Denise's penchant for good coffee and Carol's love of tasty snacks, they loved coming to the office for meetings even though they felt they had little relevant information to offer. They felt like shags on a rock. They'd been watching Stranger for two weeks as a team and had very little to report. Janet and Marcia arrived on time and met Brian for the first time. They shook hands and introduced themselves as Denise and Carol entered the room.

Denise started proceedings and uncovered the white board with a flourish.

She told the meeting, "I have spoken to my husband and he told me that cases can turn overnight and that the trick is aligning all Intel gathered to form a hypothesis."

She and Carol were almost obsessed with confidentiality and dutifully covered the white board when not using it. Carol had to use her persuasive powers to convince Denise that inviting the girls to their closed shop meetings would be a positive step.

She argued, "Janet and Marcia have a vested interest in the case and have been up close and personal with the target."

Denise eventually capitulated after she'd discussed the situation with her husband, ex homicide cop Don.

He advised, "The best information I received when on active duty came from criminals close to a source."

The trick was piecing the information together to make sense.

The girls sat up the back as all newbies do at meetings. They looked a little uncomfortable, but after introductions and coffees were made, they settled in and studied the board in front of them. All the surveillance that they'd completed over the last three months was grouped in relevant sections with a timeline with dates and times. Rosslyn and Richmond were in attendance and all photos and film taken by Rosslyn were shown to a captivated audience. It was all there. The hours and months of surveillance were in front of them. Everyone in the room was sworn to secrecy as some of the clues were obtained illegally. Denise did not hold back, she commenced with the illegal entry of Stranger's house and the information of child abuse and pornographic images that were sighted by Jed at the time, adding that police found no evidence on his computer after they raided his place the next day. It took Denise over two hours to cover all the information gleaned. Rosslyn's pictures showed the surveillance from the Criterion Hotel and Fortitude Valley. They broke for lunch and resumed at two p.m.

Carol took the next session and opened the floor for any questions or observations. Rosslyn took the floor, indicating who was in the photos at the Criterion Hotel and that they thought one of the photos from Fortitude Valley was of the body found at

Capalaba. The photo of the murdered parolee, Michelle Farmer, who was one of their missing person's cases was on display. Margo had confirmed the identity of Michelle and advised her family interstate had been informed of her demise. She also advised that Katherine Pierce was under close scrutiny by her case manager and had been supplying clean urine samples. She added that she had no contact with Stranger over the previous month. Kathryn reiterated the status of the current charges against Stranger, which had been dropped due to not enough evidence. Since the charges were dropped, she had no further news or contact with him.

Janet and Marcia were amazed at the images before them. Janet clearly saw herself at the Criterion Hotel and they had good shots of Fortitude Valley where she and Marcia had been trying to find out information for Hargreaves and Plummer. Marcia saw the area near Carbrook where he was observed launching a boat. Rosslyn apologised for the unclear image as they could not identify the boat. Marcia was the first one to speak. She told the meeting this place was one of the places Stranger had shown them on their fishing trip. She'd taken photos with her little digital camera during that day and showed the places of interest that he had outlined and had nice clear photos of the boat, including the registration number. Denise immediately left the room and was back in ten minutes. They now knew who owned the boat. He was identified as Jack Donnelly of Capalaba. He was known as the best fence in Brisbane in his time. Hell, he'd used that boat and others to rob and steal from waterside properties. Not that he did the dirty work himself. He was well liked within the criminal fraternity and had no trouble enlisting thieves to steal on order. That's why he was a good fence. He'd have the goods moved on often before they were reported missing or stolen.

Marcia was quite chuffed with herself and the response she got from everyone in the room.

Janet, on the other hand, appeared to be in deep thought. *Christ*, she thought *the Wii games and computer Stranger gave her boys fitted into the timeline. It had crashed a few times and was now useless; she had to hire one to enable her boys to play their games.* She did not want to steal Marcia's thunder but had to say something. She now told the meeting about the computer that was now in the repair shop. She also added that Stranger and Holly wanted them to go fishing overnight. The girls both added that they had recognised Holly and lonely boy from the club at the Gold Coast.

Marcia insisted, "He left with Holly that night."

She remembered the police raid occurring after Holly had left that night.

Denise and Carol looked at each other and shook their heads. From the feeling that the investigation was going nowhere, to the bombshells the girls dropped. Hell, they'd identified the boat, areas on the waterways that were significant, Stranger's daughter, Holly, with their missing person. All progress was due to inviting the girls to the meeting. Though the progress was significant, it would not be enough to prosecute or convict anyone at this time.

The next question was would they let the girls go on an overnight trip on the boat. The answer was yes, they would, as Carol indicated there'd be no stopping them. The girls agreed to wait for an invitation from Stranger. Jed and Brian promised to continue watching him and would stay close. They indicated they'd like to utilise Rosslyn and Richmond in their surveillance. Rosslyn would be utilised for her photography skills and Richmond for his sixth sense of impending danger. Everyone agreed to keep their ears and eyes open.

Chapter Forty-Five

Carol insisted on calling Winter and Autumn by their real names during the meeting. Marcia and Janet left the meeting and felt like real grownups. They liked being treated as equals. Janet told the meeting she'd retrieve her old computer from the repair shop, where she had left it when it crashed. Hell, she had not bothered to check whether it had been fixed as she had forgotten about it as she had rented another computer for six months.

They left Hargreaves and Plummer at four-thirty p.m. when Janet's phone rang.

Marcia answered it, saying, "Marcia speaking."

There was a pause at the other end, then she heard Stranger's voice ask, "Who am I speaking to?"

Marcia said, "You called me, who am I speaking to?"

Stranger identified himself and Marcia replied that she would get Autumn, aka Janet, to the phone. Janet was her convivial self over the phone. She'd told Stranger they were in Capalaba on their way to the Tavern. He'd agreed to meet them there in about thirty minutes and would be bringing Holly. Marcia became tetchy. She was looking around as Janet was talking, trying to see whether Stranger was in the vicinity. She signalled Janet to keep walking as they were in front of the office. Janet nodded that she understood and scooted out to the car park and got into the car. They went straight to the Koala Tavern and were drinking a bourbon and playing the pokies when Stranger arrived half an hour later.

As Stranger approached, he had a querulous look in his eyes, they were inscrutable and when he said, "Marcy, Marcy, Marcy," Marcia felt extremely uncomfortable and felt she was being stripped in public. She had been introduced to him as Winter when at the Gold Coast.

He was undressing her with his eyes. Her smile did not reach her eyes as she greeted Stranger jovially enough and even cracked a joke about being found out. Janet nearly choked on her drink as Marcia explained not many people knew her real name, or Janet's for that matter. She laughed it off and excused herself so she could have a cigarette in the smoking area of the pub. She had that feeling that most criminals know well. She felt the fluttery tummy, pain in the guts, and a tightening of one's arse. She could not shake these feelings as Stranger followed her to the smoking area. She knew this feeling came from the fear of being found out, the fear of knowing who to trust. Trust no one but yourself was the usual survival technique but, in reality, you had to trust someone. Marcia realised the only ones she trusted were Janet and the crew at Hargreaves and Plummer.

As they sat in communicable silence, puffing on their smokes, Stranger nodded and said, "I know how you feel, Marcy."

Marcia was taken aback by the familiarity of his words but remained silent. It's a matter of trust. She had not been keen on the overnight fishing expedition, and when Stranger mentioned it to her, she felt she could express her unwillingness to go.

She started by saying, "I enjoyed the daytime trip and I am willing to go on another trip with you, Holly and Janet."

She plucked up the courage and told him truth, "I do not like roughing it to the extent that I think the boat will be overcrowded for a sleep over."

She added, "I don't like being eaten alive by midges and mosquitoes and I am frightened about fishing or crabbing in the dark."

Stranger let her finish and agreed with her. He told her that Holly and Janet were the only ones that thought it was a good idea and he'd only agreed to please his daughter. They began to relax and agreed a daytime trip in good weather would be a better idea and more enjoyable. They were confident they could get Janet and Holly to agree with them as they both could be persuasive.

Stranger casually asked, "What have you been up to?"

Marcia felt herself blanch but quickly pulled herself together. She told him that her and Janet have been spending time shopping, going to movies, drinking, and gambling in that order. She indicated that Janet has another eight days of freedom without her kids, and they were making up for lost time. She reflected on them aimlessly filling time and felt deeply embarrassed about wasting precious time. She could hardly tell him their true mission. That they were working undercover for Hargreaves and Plummer to get close to their target, him. She couldn't really tell him about her source of income as a drug dealer, as she wanted his approval even though she was scared of him on a subliminal level. But within herself, she would not lose focus on their original motive of seeking revenge or justice for their murdered friend. She knew that to trick a trickster she would have to stay in control and would discuss this issue with Janet when she was sober and straight.

When they returned to the pokies, Janet and Holly were playing together, raising and lowering the bet and squealing with delight when they got the free spin or feature when they had maximised their bet. They'd won over a thousand dollars and were about to plunge it back through the machine when Stranger rescued them by telling them to keep their money as they were going to shout dinner and drinks for them all. Holly could see the sense in this and cashed in the ticket and proceeded to the restaurant. They ordered the best and most expensive food and drinks. They all had a good time, even though the food was still average, and agreed to go on their next fishing trip during the day. Stranger agreed to phone Janet to make the arrangement. Stranger agreed to check the weather forecast and would pick one of those days in Queensland when it would be sunny and warm. Marcia and Stranger were carefully watching each other and their drinks. They both were driving and proceeded to engage in polite conversation as Holly and Janet got hammered and chatted ceaselessly about past conquests, the things they'd got away with, and the upcoming picnic and fishing trip.

Marcia literally rolled Janet into the car and saw with great amusement that Stranger was having the same difficulty with Holly. As they waved goodbye to each other, Marcia was muttering under her breath and chided Janet about her level of intoxication and subsequent behaviour.

She dropped her home and told her, "I'll see you tomorrow at noon."

As they needed to make plans and a list of things to do before meeting Stranger and Holly again.

Stranger drove straight home and helped Holly to bed in that he put her on the bed fully dressed and placed a doona over her. She'd literally passed out by the time they arrived home. He'd have to talk to her tomorrow. He wanted to know more about the girls. Hell, he thought, the only thing he knew about them was they were known convicted criminals. Even though he associated more with Janet, he felt he had a connection with Marcia and began fantasying about having a real and proper relationship with her. She was not bad looking, had no kids, and was the most sensible person he had met in years. He felt attracted to her.

Chapter Forty-Six

Jed and Brian were in position when Stranger and his daughter arrived home. They looked at the heavy black cloud overhead and cursed under their breaths. Bloody Queensland weather, beautiful one day, pitiful the next, as the saying went. According to Brian, it had been pitiful for the last three days, heavy torrential rain as predicted. Brian now knew why Carol had pulled out of the surveillance of Stranger's house. Now he had to suffer the bities when lying in the mulch and undergrowth.

They watched as Stranger manhandled Holly out of the car and up the front steps as she was hopelessly drunk. Brian became fascinated by the sight of her and longed to get hammered. He hadn't had a drink for over a month as Jed had let him know in no uncertain terms that his employment depended on his sobriety. However, watching Holly made him long and hunger for a drink and reminded him of the Pretenders song, 'Some of us lying in the gutter, some of us looking at the stars'. That's where he'd been before Jed offered him the job. Broke and in the gutter. His situation was slowly improving since becoming sober. Holly appeared to be a happy drunk, not like him. He knew he was nasty and prone to violence. As they both stumbled toward the house, he was daydreaming about what the name of the song was. 'Talk of the Town' or 'Back on a Chain Gang'. He chuckled to himself, or so he thought. Jed gave him a look that would kill as Stranger suddenly turned around and was looking in their direction. Holly, on the other hand, had turned from happy to belligerent in a split second, complaining and ready to pick a fight. She did not like being manhandled. Stranger knew intuitively how to handle her as he let her go and allowed her to stumble and fall. As she pulled herself up off the floor and managed to get up the stairs, she gave a triumphant look as she entered the lounge room. Stranger knew to let her be and watched as she ricocheted off the walls, knocking over things as she made her way to her room. He heard a few more crashing noises and decided to check on her later.

Christ, he hated drunks and the sound of things breaking. It made him think of his upbringing, which reminded him of the saying, 'I wasn't brought up, I was thrown against the wall and told to get up'. He hated his father the most, the breaker of all things precious to him. He only felt contempt for his mother, who suffered in silence for most of her married life but became more assertive and nastier after the old man was retrenched or sacked after punching out a work mate. He knew how love turns to hate, and by the time these two departed this life in a house fire, they had actively hated each other. They say it started with a cigarette. He knew it started with a cigarette. It was an experiment. At the time, he had been working for a construction company who sent all staff to a fire safety course to fulfil workplace health and safety requirements. The fireman who facilitated the course showed a video of how fire spreads and how easily furniture and carpet caught alight. It was magnificent how quickly fire spreads. He'd visited his aging parents long before his conviction and prison sentence. He remembered the visit being strained due to their broken relationship. His father spoke to his mother like a piece of shit, and she reciprocated in like manner, and she knew she could get away with it. His father was too ill and sick to look after himself and had to cop it sweet. He now understood this type of relationship as a co-dependency of sorts. When he left their house, he left a burning cigarette between the cushions on the lounge and drove straight home, daydreaming about the catastrophic fire that would follow.

In his mind, he rehearsed his response to the media, one of solemn shock with a few tears for good measure. The fire was reported on the news that night. The spokesman for the fire brigade made a statement that there were no suspicious circumstances and it appeared to have been started by a cigarette in the lounge room. The neighbours reported on their valiant efforts to rescue the old couple but were driven back by the smoke and the heat. One of the neighbours added they were a lovely couple and good neighbours. *Pig's arse*, Stranger thought at the time. No one asked the question were they smokers. They were at one time but were reformed smokers who would not allow the smoking of cigarettes in their house. No one asked how or why the fire started and no one from the media contacted him, so his prepared response was not needed or required. He raided their bank account to pay for the funeral. He went for the cheapest option, had them cremated, and was not surprised when no one came to the service. What did surprise him, however, was the amount of money they had in the bank at the time of their deaths. He inherited everything, sold the property, and with the proceeds and the money in the bank, bought a rural property at Gatton. He still owned the property, which had a modest house on eight acres, enough room for privacy. He left all his trophies there and was sure no one knew the location or his connection to the property as he only went there when he had employment in the area.

He continued to daydream and fantasise about Marcia as he sat on his patio that overlooked the garden. His saw lights at the end of the driveway as heavy rain began to fall; he then remembered the noise he heard when he arrived home. He continued to see lights and decided to get his LED torch, raincoat, and hat to investigate. Jed and Brian had left their positions when the rain started as they saw no value in getting wet. They were crouching down and on the move when they saw the beam of light shining down on the end of the driveway. Stranger was approaching and they had to change direction and scurry out another way. Christ, they were nearly caught; the only reason they weren't seen was due to the fact that Stranger was focussing his torch toward the end of the driveway. As they got into Jed's wife's Hyundai Excel, Jed cursed as he noticed they were covered in mud and dripping wet. Elaine would be cranky. He'd have to have the car professionally detailed and cleaned or he'd have to face a tongue lashing when he got home. For all Jed's SAS training and previous combat experience, the skills which he utilised at work, he knew his wife's opprobrium would unsettle and upset his home life. He was tough but his wife could become nasty and vicious if she knew what he had been doing in her car. Christ, he was under her thumb, so to speak, and the only one who knew or noticed the toxicity of their relationship was Carol. He'd told her of his situation at home in an unguarded moment, and since she had been aware, she noticed the dynamic between them and always communicated with Elaine in a cheerful and inclusive manner. Carol knew what pissed Elaine off was not being told the truth and did not like being lied to or lied to by omission. She was a drunk who ruled the roost at home.

He'd drop Brian off and get the car cleaned before he returned home. Brian, on the other hand, was daydreaming of getting hammered and his thoughts drifted to the Pretenders song and Chrissie Hynde. He now thought the song was 'Message of Love' and realised Marcia looked like her. He was thinking of

Marcia, she was single and so was he; he began to think of omens and love when Jed dropped him at his place. As Brian got out of the car, he realised he had nothing to go home to, no one to love and care for him. He began to fantasise about how he would capture Marcia's heart.

Stranger spent a few minutes looking at the lights at the end of his driveway and realised they were fairy lights or phosphorous, he then noticed the ground was disturbed. He felt sure someone had been watching him as he returned to the house.

Chapter Forty-Seven

Marcia woke up early the next day and was feeling anxious and nervous about the familiarity Stranger had shown her at the Tavern the night before. *Familiarity breeds contempt*, she thought. As she arranged her thoughts, she thought of Carol's advice years ago when she was trying to teach her decision making, using the for and against argument, make the decision, and then make a plan. She began brainstorming and listing what she needed to prioritise. She found it slightly amusing playing undercover agent, the closer she became to the targets, the more she began to feel fear and foreboding. After last night's efforts at the Tavern, Marcia was appalled by Janet and Holly's level of intoxication and knew she would have to confront Janet and remind her to remain in control. As they had work to do to further the investigation of their friend's so-called suicide, she rang Carol at home and arranged to see her and Denise at the office at Capalaba after nine a.m.

Marcia arrived on time and was shown through to the meeting room by Rosslyn, who was manning reception with Richmond, who was fast asleep under her desk. Jed and Brian were already there and were helping themselves to coffee as Marcia entered the room. Brian almost choked and spat coffee over the front of his white t-shirt. He'd had a long, soaking bath when he got home the night before and was having unclean thoughts of Marcia and how he would romance and seduce her. Shit, she does look like Chrissie Hynde in person. She smiled at him and had an amused look on her face that travelled to her eyes. He looked up sheepishly as he tried to wipe off the coffee from his t-shirt. It only made it worse. Marcia ordered him to take off his t-shirt so she could soak it in bleach in the sink in the kitchen. Once he had his shirt off, Marcia could not help herself, she had a good look at him. She had met him for the first time at yesterday's meeting and was so focussed on her so-called presentation on the trip to the Gold Coast that she failed to recognise what a good sort Brian was. Military-style haircut, mostly good body, nice hands, and lovely brown eyes. She felt comfortable around him, and her fearfulness and anxiety dissipated as she continued to check him out.

Carol looked on quizzically at the scene in the meeting room as Marcia brushed past carrying Brian's t-shirt, heading towards the kitchen. As she passed Rosslyn she asked whether they had any bleach. Rosslyn told her to look under the sink or in the shower, laughed, and commented on Marcia's mothering instinct. As she was soaking the t-shirt, Marcia began to relax. She always felt safe at the office and genuinely liked the crew that worked there, including Denise. She thought, *fuck the mothering instinct, he is cute*. She giggled as she rinsed the t-shirt, and had carnal instinct and thoughts towards Brian.

When she returned to the meeting room, the boys were telling Denise and Carol about last night's surveillance and, without dobbing each other in, how they were nearly caught by Stranger. Both Brian and Jed felt to continue observing the target at close quarters was becoming counterproductive as he had ceased his midnight excursions to Fortitude Valley. The boys did not mention the bities, rain, and how uncomfortable this surveillance had become as they did not like to whinge or appear to be soft. Brian suggested putting a tracking device on Stranger's vehicle to enable them to follow him.

He claimed, "I am an expert in tracking devices."

And suggested putting one on the boat as they knew he used the boat on a few occasions and their failure at these times was the inability to follow him.

When Marcia returned from the kitchen, Denise announced, "Here comes the washer woman."

And smirked as everyone in the room burst out laughing at her discomfort and the look on her face. Brian was grinning and sitting with a jacket over his bare chest. Marcia took the stir in good humour and had one last peek at Brian's bare chest, not too hairy with a manly physique. She cleared her throat before she explained why she was there.

She said, "Me and Janet met up with Stranger at the Tavern last night."

She explained how she felt at the time and described her feelings of trepidation when she was in his company. She advised the meeting that she and Janet were too scared to go boating at night with him and Holly.

She then added, "Janet and Holly got uproariously drunk, and this added to my discomfort as me and Stranger were sober and the vibe he puts out is creepy."

She had to admit to everyone present that she was scared of him and was losing her nerve for undercover work.

She told them, "Stranger has agreed to a daytime trip in the boat once the weather clears up."

And admitted that she was a fair-weather sailor and would only go out on a perfect day.

She said, "We have not had a chance to track down Janet's computer as we were distracted by Stranger's phone call and had arranged to go to the pub for tea."

Marcia admitted to being a party girl in the past but was over it and had to admit she hated drunks and drug taking party animals.

She added, "Holly was as scary as her father and Janet knows no boundaries once she starts on her coke-fuelled alcohol binges."

After she completed her diatribe, she looked around and everyone was nodding in agreement. She felt relieved to get it off her chest.

She said, "I have to pick up Janet, to retrieve the computer from the repair shop, and will bring it round so it can be checked by Denise's IT friends within the Queensland Police Service."

Denise had been busy since yesterday's meeting and advised that there was footage of the police raid at the club at Surfers Paradise and the missing boy could be seen leaving with Holly, who had been identified by her. However, no trace of the boy had been found. They all agreed to Brian's idea of tracking devices on both vehicles, his Ford Territory and Jack Donnelly's boat, and allocated the tasks of surveillance based on skills. Rosslyn, Carol, and Richmond would follow the boat due to Rosslyn's knowledge of the waterways between Redland Bay and the Gold Coast. Jed and Brian would follow his vehicle. Denise would co-ordinate all surveillance and liaise with the police. She would arrange the tracking devices and organise the whole operation from the office.

Chapter Forty-Eight

Stranger was up early the following morning and returned to the bottom of the driveway. His thoughts returned to last night and how tetchy he felt when he first saw the lights. He had convinced himself he was being watched and was relieved when he observed the glowing phosphorous. No wonder people believed in fairies as it took him a good five minutes to figure out what he was looking at. In the cold heart of day, however, what he was looking at reinforced his paranoia. The ground had been disturbed, flattened in places, and he swore he could see muddy footprints or rather drag marks that led to the street. He decided to act on his feelings and would set up sensor security lights that would come on if someone was in his yard. He needed to clear up some loose ends and had stayed up late trying to figure out where he went wrong and the solution to his mistakes. He'd have to get his computer back from Janet and would have to travel to Gatton to clean up the trophy site. He left a note for Holly, letting her know he'd gone out and would be back soon, and decided he would pop into Janet's and retrieve his computer. After he had his breakfast, he went straight to Bunning's at Capalaba. He was glad they opened early. A staff member showed him which aisle the sensor lights were kept but had no advice on how to set them up. 'The directions are on the packet' was the only advice they could give. He knew that of course and read the packets carefully before he made his selection. Packers and stackers were all they were, with no clue of what they were selling. He could always get the lights installed if he could not do it himself.

When he arrived at Janet's, he could smell the big breakfast she was cooking emanating through the front door. He was sorry he had toast for breakfast. She seemed surprised when she answered the door, did not appear any worse for wear, and offered him a coffee, which he accepted gratefully. After the downpour from the previous night, the weather was still overcast and cloudy.

He asked for his computer, and without skipping a beat, Janet told him. "I had a break in, and it was stolen along with the games, my iPad, and phone."

"I had to rent a new one from Rentlo as the computer games were the only things that kept the boys quiet," she flippantly added. "I did not report the matter to police because I know that it would do no good and I don't want any contact with them due to my history."

He nodded in understanding and hoped that whoever stole it took it for their own use and had not hocked it at Cash Converters. Janet felt her gut wrench as she handed him his coffee.

Her hand was shaking slightly, and she gave him a sheepish look and muttered, "I must have had too much alcohol last night."

She enquired, "How did Holly pull up?"

Stranger laughed and said, "She was cactus and was still in bed when I left home this morning."

Janet, on the other hand, was in pretty good shape and ate her bacon, eggs, tomatoes, and mushrooms with relish as they discussed their next outing, either a fishing trip or more clubbing, Stranger was not sure.

What he was sure about was that he needed more cocaine to appease his daughter's appetite. He wanted Janet to score for him as he did not like scoring drugs.

She laughed and told him, "Whilst I will participate in drug use, I am reluctant to score powder from anyone as it would jeopardise my family."

She would, however, arrange a deal with Dianne so he could pick up somewhere else and not at her home.

Stranger was happy with this arrangement. They continued chatting about last night, the upcoming fishing trip, and Marcia's fear of going out on boats at night.

He asked, "Does Marcia have a boyfriend or any family?"

Janet's lie came trippingly off her lips, yes, she has a boyfriend. A lie. And yes, she has two adult children and five grandchildren who all live in regional New South Wales whom she makes an effort to visit once a year and she never forgets their birthdays. That was true. He asked about her boyfriend.

Janet said, "To tell you the truth, I've never met him but according to Marcia he is cute."

And she left it at that for the moment. Stranger commented that he can't be that committed or was not a jealous guy if he let her go clubbing and gallivanting about with her girlfriends. He now knew why she appeared sensible and more responsible than Janet; it was because she was loved by many.

Janet changed the topic and the focus returned to how his back was going and did his workers' compensation come through as she knew he liked talking about himself. He claimed his back was still giving him gyp, a lie as far as Janet had observed, and that he was still being paid sick leave and expected no problems with workers' compensation once he had seen the good doctor, who would extend his medical certificate and time off. They both laughed simultaneously. Janet, in her muddled state of mind, thought they actually got on well, but not as girlfriend or

166

boyfriend. She shuddered after he left, what would she tell Marcia? She'd have to tell her the truth and the lies and knew her friend might go ape shit, but then again, she might not as she was more mature than me. *I'm the one with unresolved issues with boundaries, as Carol used to tell me.* She never really knew what she meant, but now felt she understood.

Brian picked up the tracking devices and went straight to Stranger's house. He was not at home, so he attached the B tracker to Jack's boat. He decided to attach the A tracker to his Ford Territory at a later date as he and Jed had no intention of returning to night surveillance at the house. It would be more exciting to pursue than to watch. They figured they could attach the tracker anytime, anyplace.

Stranger's car arrived at the house as Brian was leaving. Two close calls in two days. They'd have to be more careful. When he entered the house, there was no sign of Holly. She was still in bed and the room smelt of vomit. He set to work on the security lights.

Chapter Forty-Nine

Marcia arrived on time at noon. Janet was having a coffee and a smoke on her back veranda. There were no signs of a hangover. It was obvious that she'd got up early as her house was spick and span, with the added smell of Domestos, lemon air freshener, and furniture polish. Marcia liked the smell of a clean house and was surprised Janet was in a good enough shape to do it after last night's efforts.

Janet offered her coffee and told her she'd had a visit from Stranger earlier that day and he was fishing for information about her. She relayed the whole conversation and told Marcia she said she has a boyfriend. Marcia could feel her blood pressure rising, she hated people or anyone knowing her private details, especially Stranger. She knew his name was Peter but would continue calling him Stranger as it depersonalised the relationship. She would prefer he still thought of her as Winter, not Marcia.

She did not drink her coffee and got up abruptly to indicate they were leaving to retrieve the computer from the shop at Capalaba where Janet had left it to be fixed. They arrived at the shop within minutes to find that the guy who ran it was about to close up.

Janet rushed in before he closed and asked, "Have you still got my computer that I left here to be repaired?"

He told her, "There was nothing wrong with it, or rather your kids must have disabled it by hitting the wrong button."

He said she could not retrieve it as he had sold it. He reckoned he'd told her that he had a fourteen day turn around, and seeing that she did not pick it up, it was his to sell. Janet was about to go ballistic when Marcia came in and calmed the situation down. She told the guy that Janet had disabled or special needs children who needed the computer as gaming was the only thing that calmed them down. He told her that he had sold it to a single mum for two hundred and fifty dollars and wondered out loud if he could possibly give them her address so they could try to get it back for Janet's kids. He gave Marcia the buyers details and said it was usual for gamers to have no knowledge of how computers worked, and that he had fixed a few in his time that had nothing wrong with them but were incapacitated by those who had trouble uploading or downloading games.

Janet explained, "I have not been back to pick it up as I rented one in the interim and had a six-month contract. I completely forgot about the fourteen-day pick up."

She realised she had not given him a contact number as she thought she would return within that time. However, she now realised that she and Marcia had been side-tracked with the undercover arrangement.

They went around to the address supplied which was located in a housing commission area near Victoria Point. There was no one home. Janet put on some gloves and started checking doors and windows to see if any were unlocked. Marcia was gobsmacked and asked Janet what she thought she was doing.

Janet turned, smiled, and said, "Just a bit of breaking and entering, just like the old days."

"Yeah, right," said Marcia. "The good old days when you were off your face, out of control, thieving things, and breaking into houses. That ended up with you in prison for a few years due to your prior history."

Janet found the back door unlocked and was about to enter when a car pulled up in the driveway. Marcia was you-hooing and shouting 'anyone home'. Janet stopped what she was about to do and was you-hooing as the occupant of the house, Natalie Smith, and her kids were getting out of the car, retrieving the weekly grocery shop from the boot. Natalie looked at them suspiciously. What were these two women doing around the side of the house? Marcia took over and explained herself succinctly. It started to shower rain again and Natalie invited them in for coffee as they assisted with the unloading of the groceries. Natalie sussed they were all right, due to their 'rock chicks from the seventies' look that they maintained. Nice threads, good quality jeans and boots. As they were drinking their coffees and admiring Natalie's house, Marcia explained that Janet needed the computer for her autistic child, who had been hospitalised with an asthma attack. Due to the drama of the sick child, she had forgotten to pick up the computer she had left for repairs to be picked up within fourteen days. Natalie appeared to sympathise but was not willing to give it back as she could not afford another one or indeed another second hand one. Marcia nodded in agreement. Janet appeared to be chewing the side of her cheek, and Marcia flashed her a look that told her to shut her mouth as she offered to buy a new laptop for seven hundred dollars. She'd seen them on special at Harvey Norman Capalaba and would be prepared to go there today. Natalie agreed without argument, and they set off for the shops after they finished their coffee. They went in Marcia's car, which was parked about five doors down the street. *Old habits die hard*, they both thought as they got into the car. In their housebreaking days it was called sneaking around. That is, you'd drive down a street, any street, and if you noticed an open front door, you'd park down the street, walk back, and rob the place. By the time they arrived at Harvey Norman, Janet had regained her composure and was chatting with Natalie like old mates. She was glad Marcia handled the sale and obtained a good deal for Natalie and her kids. They drove back to Victoria Point, dropped Natalie off, and picked up the computer. Mission accomplished as they high-fived each other when they got back to the car for a second time.

Janet was glad Marcia had handled the situation with Natalie, was calm, and listened to what Natalie needed and made an offer too good to refuse. Janet, on the other hand, was about to break into her house, and when she appeared reluctant to part with her computer, she was going to snot her but decided not to when Marcia flashed that 'don't you dare' look. They went back to Marcia's place for lunch of lasagne and salad. Marcia was a good cook and kept her unit mostly clean but not tidy. She tended to stack items in piles rather than put everything away. They were impressed with Natalie Smith's housing commission place at Victoria Point as it looked like a normal house. Marcia and Janet both lived in older housing commission areas that looked like low-income housing and attracted similar tenants, some good, and some bad. They had to put up with their neighbours' bad behaviour, drunken brawls, domestic violence, and drug use. They'd got used to it over the years as they were both long-term tenants. They would not dream of moving due to the low rent and stability of tenancy. They'd checked out the private rental market and knew the pitfalls of high rent, no stability, and the fact that if you complained or wanted any repairs done, your rent would go up or your lease would not be renewed. Natalie would be on a similar deal but in an area where they placed housing commission properties amongst or in a normal neighbourhood. They figured what's normal and were laughing and thinking it's what you get used to at the end of the day.

Speaking of normal, Janet said, "The computer problem has been solved; now I need to get you a bloke, seeing that I put you in deep shit."

Marcia knew her friend meant well but said she had someone in mind and left it at that for the time being.

Marcia pointed out bits of last night's entertainment and her observation of Holly chucking on herself and continuing drinking. They both agreed that at least she did not get nasty. 'Not a nasty drunk' could be on her gravestone. They agreed not to get into such big drinking sessions when in the company of their targets as it would be a mistake and they needed to keep their wits about them. Janet admitted to drinking in excess when she was nervous and would try to control her behaviour in the future. They had a job to do and were grateful of the rain as this meant no boat trips in the near future.

Chapter Fifty

The rain had set in., Stranger had checked the forecast and heavy rain was expected for the next week. He was cursing as he wanted and needed to set up his security lights in the garden. He would have to wait.

By the time he got back to his house, Holly was out of bed. She looked dishevelled and guilty, like one does when they can't remember getting home from the Tavern last night. Stranger was strangely quiet. He had noticed that she had changed her clothes and noticed last night's outfit was in the laundry tub. He could smell vomit. He had observed her drinking behaviour at the Tavern. Holly and Janet started on bourbon and by the end of the night they appeared to be in a competition on who could drink the most beer, drinking schooners, calling them little big girls' drinks. He noticed her vomit down the front of her jumper at the Tavern as she continued drinking beer. He observed the look on Janet's face, one of bemusement, as Holly continued drinking. Janet continued as if nothing happened. Marcia did not seem to notice but on reflection he thought she probably did but did not say anything at the time. He did the same. He thought about giving her a hard time but decided against it. He did not want to spoil what was a good night but had to remark on the clothes in the laundry tub and left it at that, he did not want to argue with his daughter. She did appear a bit embarrassed as her recollection of the night came back to her in bits and pieces, flashes of what really happened. At least her dad got her home safely and did not nag her about the state she had got herself in. She was thankful for that. The only thing he said to her was she need not try to keep up with Janet as she could drink just about anyone under the table. Stranger knew this from personal experience. They decided to veg out, eat snacks, and watch movies all day.

Stranger was disappointed finding out Marcia had a boyfriend. She had not told him, and when he thought about it, she had not told him about her kids and grandkids. The only thing he had found out was her name, which she seemed extremely upset and nervous about. He first thought she was an extremely private person, but upon reflection, he decided it's the psychological hyper-vigilance of the career criminal's mindset.

Chapter Fifty-One

Marcia phoned Carol to arrange dropping off the computer they had retrieved from Natalie at the office. When she and Janet arrived, Marcia virtually ran into Brian and nearly bowled him over. She was a bit flustered and had another good look at him. He was not bad looking, nice eyes, and she liked the fact he had a bit of a dad's body. Certainly not like Stranger, who appeared to be a gym junky trying to maintain his youth by being trim, taut, and terrific. Brian had a certain appeal, twinkling eyes when communicating with others, and a confidence of someone who was secure within themselves. How little did she know?

Denise and Carol were fussing about the office and were excited about checking the computer's hard drive. Denise had arranged an IT expert to check this out and knew nothing stays deleted and could be retrieved. He was a young policeman, compared to the old cronies at Hargreaves and Plummer, who knew these things could be done but, on the other hand, were totally clueless on where to begin. Denise and Carol waited and watched in anticipation as young Paul did his magic. Whilst Marcia, Janet, and Brian were interested, they did not hang over Paul's shoulder like Jed, Carol, and Denise. Marcia started chatting up Brian as Janet discreetly made herself invisible.

They'd found a quiet corner in the room and, for the first time in years, Marcia was talking about herself and family and listened with interest to Brian's story. She found out he was single, and divorced, with an ex-wife and three children to support. He explained they had separated and were later divorced due to his excessive use of alcohol, he admitted he was an alcoholic on the dry. This was a little too much information for Marcia, she thought she did not need to take on anyone else's baggage at this point in time. She was, however, appreciative of his honesty. She was not sure whether to become involved with someone who would be prone to lapses in abstinence as she knew from past experience how things could turn out badly. She had to ask herself, would she be willing to take the risk, or would she use him to alleviate her situation and the apprehensive feeling she had towards Stranger. She decided instantaneously that she would utilise Brian in the interim to enable herself some time and space in keeping Stranger at bay. She thanked Brian for his honesty and then outlined her plan to him. She admitted that she would like to use him as her current boyfriend to excuse herself from Stranger's grasp as he gave her the creeps. She now felt unsure whether Brian would go for it.

Brian was gobsmacked by her honesty and told her, "I would love to play the part of your current boyfriend."

And then he asked her out for dinner that night. She accepted and he arranged to pick her up at her place at seven p.m. They both appeared happy with the arrangement and Marcia left Hargreaves and Plummer with Janet.

Marcia told Janet of her date with Brian and how he had agreed to play her current boyfriend. Janet laughed and chided her friend to be careful and not fall in love. They both laughed at the thought of being in love with someone and reflected on their past experiences in love, which all ended in disaster. They were both good at picking damaged goods that had disastrous results to their self-esteem and confidence. That's one of the reasons they remained single, the other reason was that they liked their independence and freedom of choice. They both hated being told what to do with their lives, and as soon as anyone thought they could tell them what to do, that was the usual death knell for the relationship. As Marcia dropped Janet off, she agreed to let her know how the dinner date went with Brian that night.

By the time Brian left Hargreaves and Plummer, the computer expert had not retrieved anything meaningful from the computer hard drive. Brian had a few things to do and went straight to Stranger's house to attach a tracking device to his Ford Territory and left without being seen. He knew he was good at sneaking in and out and observed that Stranger and Holly were engrossed in watching a movie. He then contacted Denise to inform her that both the boat and truck were tagged and that she could now activate her GPS program on her computer.

Brian then went home and cleaned up his flat to keep busy and to help keep his mind off Marcia. He was surprised with her honesty and was enamoured by her charm and good looks. He knew the current boyfriend status was a sham, but he was willing to take the risk and dreamt it could turn into a loving, meaningful meeting of the minds, a lover's tryst. He ironed his best set of clothes, had a long bath and, thought on how hard it was to remain sober. In the past, he had relied on alcohol to lubricate his confidence and was usually three sheets to the wind before going on a date. He had always felt awkward in social settings, and though he knew he was not bad looking, he felt inferior to other people. He had sobered up but these feelings of inadequacy and his fragile mental state when criticized plagued his feelings of uncertainty. Marcia was the first person in years that he felt comfortable with, and he decided he was going to go all out to impress her, but knew he could not fake it as she appeared to have an inborn antenna for bullshit. He was not even sure where to take her. He knew he could not take her anywhere flash or pretentious or to the Tavern, as it would remind her of Stranger. He decided on the Mexican place at Capalaba but would let her choose where to go. He laughed at himself in the mirror at the chicken he had become and realised he had not asked her where she lived as he already knew. He wondered whether she would find it strange that he knew her address. He felt ashamed and a bit like a stalker and was hoping she'd not notice he knew where she lived without asking her and hoped she would assume Jed had told him her address. He picked her up on time and was pleased she was ready. He was also glad he was not overdressed. She wore designer jeans and a black t-shirt with a nice, good quality leather jacket. She seemed pleased that he suggested the Mexican restaurant. Their dinner date went well, the food was nice, and he felt comfortable in her company. She was happy to drink coke with her meal. They kept the conversation casual and chatted about music they liked and concerts they had attended in the past. They liked a lot of the same bands and music. They had a lot of things in common and laughed at the same things. The time flew and when he dropped her home, she asked him how he knew where she lived. It was the moment of truth, should he tell her the truth or should he lie. He decided on the truth and told her he had found out her address as he thought she was cute and was considering asking her for a date. She gave him a kiss and told him she thought he was cute and was considering asking him for a date too. She told him she had a wonderful time and they exchanged phone numbers. He left feeling uplifted and almost skipped to his car. Marcia went inside and poured herself a bourbon and coke and was humming to herself when the phone rang.

It was Janet on the phone and Marcia thought she was calling about her date with Brian, but her mood was fouled when Janet told her that Stranger had called to arrange a fishing trip the next day.

She told Janet, "We'll have to go but I do not like the short notice."

Janet explained that he'd called earlier in the evening, and she did not want to ruin her date with Brian. Janet said Stranger had checked the weather forecast and tomorrow would be sunny with no wind, and she'd told him they would meet him and Holly at Redland Bay at eight a.m.

Janet told Marcia, "I have arranged and prepared a picnic lunch."

As she knew Marcia liked a bit of notice when preparing food.

Chapter Fifty-Two

Holly and Stranger spent the day watching movies and discussing their plans for Katherine Pierce and her family. After Holly straightened up a bit, Stranger reminded her of last night's efforts and advised her not to try to keep up with Janet in drinking competitions.

He told her, "You did not make a goose of yourself, but you were fairly shitfaced when we arrived home."

Holly, of course, had vague memories of the night and could not remember coming home or even getting into bed. She was glad her father took care of her and had commented on her behaviour, he did not nag her about it.

The forecast for tomorrow was for good weather and she was keen to go boating with the girls the next day. They both agreed the girls were good value and were fun to be around. Stranger admitted to his attraction to Marcia but had since found out she had a boyfriend.

Holly laughed and said, "I could always knock him off for you to free Marcia of her commitment."

Stranger found this amusing, he thought about it for a while and told Holly, "I would rather have Marcia as a friend."

She was not the victim type they sought to manipulate, their target, Katherine Pierce, was.

They spent the day making plans as they had a lot to do before abducting their next victims. Stranger told her of his feelings of being watched and of the incident the other night and the feeling that someone had been in his home. The first job would entail installing security lights around the house and gardens. They decided it would be best to hire a professional security firm to install the fixtures properly to ensure it worked. As they brainstormed the idea, Holly suggested they install a surveillance camera so if the lights come on, they would have video evidence of the intrusion. Stranger liked this idea and wondered why he had not thought of it before. He knew why, he had not done this in the past; he did not want to capture himself on camera with some of his previous victims. Holly's antenna went up in relation to her father's worries and feelings. She knew from experience that the feeling of being watched could be paranoia or there could be a good reason. Stranger was on the same thought pattern and told her he had searched the place for bugs when these feelings were too strong to ignore and had found nothing. She thought to herself she would search the house in a few days to see if she could find any hidden cameras or listening devices. She thought, *paranoia is like a contagion, you had to be careful not to catch it.*

He told her about his property on acreage at Gatton where he had hidden all the trophies he obtained from his own victims and the nose ring from lonely boy. The planning and scheming went on all day between snacks and movies. Even though they were similar in a lot of ways, their taste in movies was quite different. He liked old movies that were well scripted that included social issues of the time. He always thought the old British movies were the best for their low budget, good story lines and content. She, on the other hand, liked action movies and scary thrillers. In between movies, they discussed their own scary thrillers and diabolical ways to torture, emotionally abuse, and murder people. They thought of cruel ways to dispose of

Katherine Pierce and her kids and decided the ultimate end for them all would be at the Gatton property. They knew that would take some time as they needed to make the preparations properly. They would plan to escape rather than be caught. As their paranoia expanded, they decided they had become too predictable with their use of vehicles. Holly was cunning and Stranger thought how lazy and predictable he had become and how lucky he had been with not being caught.

After they planned the things to be done and the timeframe they needed, Stranger phoned Janet to arrange a fishing trip for tomorrow and hoped Marcia would be able to come as he wanted to see her again. He could not accept defeat and wanted to have her for himself, he could not let her go that easily.

Chapter Fifty-Three

After Janet hung up on Stranger and made an arrangement with him for a fishing trip, she immediately phoned Carol to tell her. She gave her the time and departure place so Carol could contact Denise with the details. Janet loved an outing and busied herself in the kitchen. She had stocked up on nice nibbles, cold chicken, and salad and made up a lovely picnic lunch that was similar to the last one. She hoped it would surpass it as she liked accolades, and after receiving compliments from Stranger and Holly from the last trip, she tried to impress them again with her choices and culinary skills. She wondered whether she should include some alcohol and decided to take a couple of bottles of wine between the four of them, thinking that would not be too excessive. For herself, she would take a few joints and would share them with Holly if she could get away with it on the day. She'd play that by ear. She phoned Marcia after she had made all her preparations, and whilst Marcia did not sound enamoured, she agreed to come as they still had an agenda. Janet was dying to ask about the date with Brian but did not want to upset Marcia and knew her friend would tell her how it went when she was ready to do so.

Marcia arrived early and they had enough time to have a coffee and pack the car. Marcia did not say much about the date, other than Brian was cute. She was more focussed on what they were going to do the next day, observing activities and taking note about what was said and done during their next excursion. They were supposed to be gathering intelligence.

When they were packing the car, Janet told Marcia, "I contacted Carol last night and advised her of the upcoming trip and have given her the times and departure location at Redland Bay."

They arrived at Redland Bay on time, and true to his nature, Stranger was punctual and had the boat ready for launch. They did not see anything untoward; they knew the crew at Hargreaves and Plummer were supposed to be following Stranger, but they could not see anyone. Marcia was wondering whether Brian was nearby and thought about the connection she felt with him after last night's date.

After three days of rain, the sun was out and the day was a balmy twenty-five degrees, the water was calm, and Moreton Bay looked beautiful. As they passed by the Bay Islands, they saw schools of dolphins in the shallow water and, halfway between Macleay Island and Karragarra Island, a dugong popped its rather large head out of the water. It was magical and they all felt good omens around them. They did not put out any crab pots as it was not the crabbing season. They did, however, follow the pathway of the last boat trip, from the mouth of the Logan River, travelling past the Bay Islands, and heading towards the Gold Coast. They stopped at different locations to drop in a line and Marcia subtlety asked a few questions about specific locations Stranger had commented on when they passed by them as she needed some clarification. The location near Russell Island where he had previously said was a good place to dump bodies was nowhere near where he had originally said it was located.

He clarified and said, "The location is eight miles out from Stradbroke Island, on the shelf."

He told them, "There was a shelf that runs the length of North and South Stradbroke Island."

Instead of lunch at the Lions Park on Russell Island, they continued on to Jacob's Wells and had their picnic at a park near the foreshore. They all thought how amazing progress could be. Once a small village on mud flats, the area had been turned into a place where the rich would want to live. Just like Sanctuary Cove, which was located nearby. They knew the Queensland Government and developers had changed Port Douglas near Cairns from a sleepy fishing village to a playground for the rich, where tourism thrived, supported by good quality accommodation and restaurants. They picnicked at a well-equipped park. Janet was chuffed at the compliments she received from her friends about the food. Marcia and Stranger lingered over their glass of wine, Janet and Holly slipped away for a walk along the foreshore where they blew a joint. Holly was appreciative of Janet's thoughtfulness as she needed the extra stimulation to go with the wine she had consumed at lunch. To add to the success of the trip, they had caught some fish, flathead and whiting. When they returned from their stroll, Janet and Holly noticed Marcia and Stranger in deep conversation. Stranger had told Marcia of how he felt he was being stalked and thought someone was intruding in his yard. Marcia did not laugh or belittle him for his fears and disclosed she had been stalked in the past by a man she did not know. She told him she was so scared she contacted police who belittled her and told her that someone must like her. She told Stranger that being stalked by an unknown stranger was unsettling, and when she tried to explain the situation to her friends, they thought she was paranoid.

She said, "My friends finally believed me when the stalker drove past my place and stopped outside when I had visitors."

She had felt so unsafe, she installed a security system that included security lights and camera. She added that after the system was installed, the stalking miraculously stopped.

She told Stranger, "It was the best thing I had ever done."

Then she told him, "I never found out who or why this person chose me," she claimed. "I will never contact or report anything to police due to their lack of response and attitude towards me when I needed some help."

She told him that she had used a local firm and gave him Jed's contact number for his security firm.

After they left Jacob's Well, they travelled past the fishing huts located on South Stradbroke Island near the Gold Coast. Marcia was trying to figure out which hut Stranger had shown them on the previous trip. Marcia was thinking which hut, Holly, who was quite chilled from the wine and dope, piped up and said something about the hut that appeared run down and commented on how well set up it was on the inside. Marcia noted this comment and wondered if Hargreaves and Plummer were indeed conducting surveillance on this trip when she noticed a small dinghy with two people and a German shepherd dog on board.

When they returned to Redland Bay, Stranger and Holly bid their farewells and said they were going home as they had a few jobs to do there. Marcia was keeping a look out to see if she could see Brian or Jed as she needed to tell them about the subterfuge she had told Stranger when she told him about her security system at home. She phoned Brian to see if he was around the area as she needed to talk to him and Jed.

Brian told her, "I will see you in half an hour."

He did not tell her about the tracking devices on Stranger's vehicles as everyone was on a need-to-know basis. He and Jed were waiting on the 'all clear' from Denise, who was manning the tracking system at the office in Capalaba. They got the 'all clear' within half an hour, Denise advised them that both vehicles went home to Stranger's house and had not moved.

Janet spotted them as they approached the jetty. Marcia's heart skipped a beat. She was surprised by the feeling she got when she saw Brian. They all greeted each other jovially and decided to rendezvous at the Redland Bay Hotel. Marcia told them both what she had discussed with Stranger, who was in need of a security system as he thought he had prowlers in his yard. Janet went to the bar to buy the drinks. Marcia told them about how she had said she had a system installed by Jed's company, but she was now worried that he would check her system before contacting Jed to set up one at his place. Jed could see the dilemma straight away and arranged to set up a system the next day. Marcia was hoping he would bring Brian. Jed couldn't believe his good luck if the job came off at Stranger's. He'd be able to remove the bugs he had left on the veranda and be able to install a better system that would capture all conversation and movement at the house in real time. If they were able to set up security cameras at Strangers it would mean Marcia was a genius of subterfuge. By the time Janet returned with the drinks, Rosslyn and Carol had arrived. They were both carrying their beers and they'd left Richmond tied up out the front of the hotel. Janet bought everyone bourbons and Brian a large orange juice with a nip of vodka in it as she did not trust anyone who did not drink alcohol. One couldn't hurt or would it. Everyone was hanging on every word Marcia said about the fishing trip. She was the centre of attention which in turn peeved off Janet who was not used to being ignored. She was feeling left out and had nasty thoughts about her best friend. Then she realised that while she was getting pissed and stoned with Holly, Marcia had been on the ball and paying attention to all that was said and done. Janet had to admire her powers of observation and knew their main goal was to get some justice for their dead friend.

By the time Brian was halfway through his drink, he was feeling relaxed and put this down to being in the company of friends and Marcia. She was looking more attractive with each sip. Brian was trying not to look longingly at her as she spoke, but it was hopeless, he was smitten. As they said their farewells in the car park, Jed arranged to meet Marcia at her house the next day when he would install a surveillance system that would appease Stranger.

Chapter Fifty-Four

As soon as Stranger and Holly unhitched the boat, they packed some clothes and food to take to Gatton. They had enough supplies to last a month, even though they only intended to stay up there for a week. They'd hired a Tarago van for a month from a dodgy second-hand car dealer on the Golden Mile. His rates were reasonable; he accepted cash and asked no questions or proof of identity. He was well known to the criminal element. He was dodgy but he loved cars and the vehicles he lent or hired were in good condition.

By the time they arrived at the Gatton property, it was getting dark. The house was set on eight acres, all of it looked unloved and unkempt. They would have a lot of work to do in preparation for what they were planning. Holly was wondering what the house looked like inside and what the bed and bedding would be like; she hated filth and was very particular when it came to a clean sleeping place. She didn't have to say anything to her father as he saw the look on her face as they approached the house. He knew what she was thinking. He tried to reassure her and told her the house had a rough exterior, very plain, built of fibro, but he maintained he had always kept it clean. He told her he had bought clean linen, bedding and a couple of brand-new euro beds. He left them there the last time he came when he tidied up the yard. She shook her head and laughed.

They went inside. The house was how he had left it, clean and tidy, although it needed airing from being locked up for a few months. The furniture was new and cheap, minimalist décor, a table and four chairs, a double seater lounge, and a coffee table and a cheap stand for the DVD player and television. There were no beds in the house and Stranger produced the blow-up beds and clean bedding from the linen closet in the hallway. The walls were painted pale yellow, which was a popular colour a few decades ago. It was his mother's favourite colour, and he recoated the walls when they looked faded or dirty. The house was all electric and he turned on the fridge and cooked a simple meal of eggs and chips for their dinner. They had an early night as they were tired from the day's activities. Holly was impressed by the comfort of the blow-up bed and promised to make breakfast the next day.

The next morning, Holly was up early making her favourite breakfast. She favoured the continental breakfast of cereal, mushrooms on toast, and fresh fruit. Stranger liked to eat like this and after breakfast , he showed her around the property. It looked better in the daylight. The yard wasn't as untidy as it first seemed, there was a definite grassed area that needed cutting back, and after they completed this job, the place looked quite good. There were clumps of trees and bushes surrounding the cleared space. Only Stranger knew the secret places and he was showing his daughter the containers that were hidden behind lantana bushes that could not be seen from the road. In fact, you could not see them when standing in front of them. He showed her the set-up. The containers were aside each other and were lined with plastic, there was an anteroom between the containers that was stocked and well organised with equipment, tools, and cleaning agents.

They stopped work for lunch and discussed the plan of abducting Katherine Pierce and her family. They knew the why but had to figure out the how and when, possible consequences, and scenarios of how to cover their tracks. Stranger knew from experience that the Probation Service would issue a warrant for her arrest if she failed to her attend her scheduled appointments. He further knew that if they persisted, they would contact Centrelink who could possibly call her in for an interview. But most likely, if police were called, they would check whether her bank account had been used. Even though Holly was blonde and a few centimetres taller than Katherine Pierce, with a little planning she could be used as a decoy. All they needed was her Centrelink number, then have Holly make enquiries at her local Centrelink office to ensure staff were familiar with her and could identify her as Katherine Pierce. Stranger knew their victim would not voluntarily attend a Centrelink office. He'd have to make contact and arrange to take the family out, where he hoped he could rummage through her purse to obtain her details. They also needed an escape route. They decided to work on that after they finished lunch.

For the next few days, they worked on the escape route. They set up snares, booby traps, and wild dog traps. They set it up and had a practice run though the overgrown area near the containers, where you either got through or were trapped. They had tied branches down that, if triggered, would whack the target in the face and knock them over. It may also disorientate the target to step on a dog trap, which could do significant damage. Both of them knew the route to take and tried it successfully several times before they were satisfied with the work completed. They knew they would re-visit the area before their plan was completed and now realised that they had a fair bit of reconnaissance to complete before enacting the main plan.

Chapter Fifty-Five

Jed arrived the next day to install a security system at Marcia's house. He could not raise Brian and was accompanied by Don, who was his main installer and a qualified electrician and an expert in video equipment. They installed the equipment in four hours and left after they'd shown Marcia how to use it. They'd set up security lights that came on automatically when someone approached the house. Once the lights went on, it automatically set off the recording of any activity outside the house. Although Marcia was disappointed Brian was not there, she was impressed by their thoroughness and professionalism.

Brian, on the other hand, woke up with a hangover and had little recollection of the previous night. He'd remembered leaving the Redland Bay Hotel and picking up a bottle of vodka on the way home. He was not sure why he had done this but vaguely remembered that he had enjoyed drinking at home alone. When Marcia had phoned at lunch time to ask how he was, he felt not only sick inside, but he also felt remorse and guilt. He did not like lying to her but then again, he could not tell her the truth. He knew he sounded different, unwell even, and told her he must have picked up a bug or eaten something that was off. He had used this excuse in the past without any thought of the validity. He now felt pathetic when dragging out this old chestnut of excuses. Even though she sounded disappointed, she agreed to contact him in a few days to see how he was doing. She even offered to come over, but he refused any help and said he'd be fine in a few days. Probably in three days, the way he felt. He hadn't been this crook in years and thought remaining sober had its own setbacks and wondered to himself why did he lapse and get into an uncontrolled drinking session alone. He'd only stopped when he'd finished the bottle, spewed, and ricocheted off a few walls on his way to bed. At least he made it to bed.

Denise and Carol were discussing their next move to escalate the case against Stranger. There had been no movement of vehicles overnight and Paul was unable to find anything incriminating on the hard drive of Janet's computer. He advised them the serial number off the hard drive did not match the computer and it appeared to have been replaced with another one that had no incriminating evidence. A games machine, as far as he was concerned, he was apologetic that he could not assist them any further. This information was disappointing; all they had now was the tracking devices, which identified no movement at his house.

Jed phoned to advise that he had installed a system at Marcia's and had not heard from Stranger but added he did not expect to hear from him for a few days. It was now a waiting game.

Denise was contacted by the Gold Coast Police, who had obtained the surveillance footage from the night club. She and Carol drove down the coast to view the footage. They could clearly see that lonely boy left the club before the raid with a tall blonde woman. The police were unable to identify the woman and were unconcerned about the missing person. Even though he was identified by Denise as the missing runaway they had pursued a few months previously, they had to admit to police that he wanted no contact with his family. They felt frustrated and knew they did not have enough evidence to pursue the matter.

They still had nothing on Stranger, even though intuitively they knew his daughter may have murdered lonely boy. But again, they had no evidence, they didn't even know the whereabouts of Stranger as his vehicle had not moved. Denise decided to send the boys, Jed and Brian, to check on Stranger's whereabouts as she was reluctant to contact ANCOR due to past experience with Constable Jones.

Chapter Fifty-Six

Marcia and Janet met for lunch at the Mexican restaurant at Capalaba. They had to admit they were bored. After the stimulation and excitement of working undercover, clubbing, and subsequent fishing expeditions, they felt down, not quite depressed, but feeling the low ebb after the stimulation of the events of the previous week. As they tucked into nachos and bean dip, they decided to visit Katherine Pierce to give her the heads up on Stranger. Janet was convinced she was in danger but had not had any time during the last month to see or convince her as they had their own worries with their outstanding charges that were now dropped. They decided to drop in on speculation after lunch. It was something constructive to do; they did not like the waiting game.

When they arrived at the Morningside address, the house looked deserted and there appeared to be no movement inside. Marcia did not know Katherine Pierce very well and, as they looked through the windows, she was surprised at the chaos and filth inside the house. Marcia thought the occupants must have left in a hurry. Janet knew that they were probably at home, playing on computers or I-pads. Janet knocked on the front door and made such a racket that Katherine Pierce eventually answered dressed in pyjamas. She sighed as she let them in. The place was a dump; she took untidiness to a new level. Marcia reluctantly accepted a coffee after washing the cup. Janet made herself at home and comfortable on a spare piece of space on the lounge after shoving the detritus to one side. Janet came straight to the point, for the purpose of their visit, giving a dire warning to the dangerousness of Stranger. Katherine virtually laughed in her face, claiming she had not seen him for at least a month, and he had been nothing but nice and kind to her and the kids. Her biggest worry at the moment was her bitch of a probation officer in Brisbane. She was tired of the scrutiny from her supervising officer as she was conducting random house checks, drug tests, and demanding to see payslips as proof of employment.

Katherine said, "I'm over it and I am considering doing a runner."

She asked Janet, "What would be the consequences if I did this?"

Janet and Marcia both agreed and told her that, "If you went interstate, your chances of not being caught would be good."

Janet and Marcia both knew of someone who had left Queensland for Tasmania that was never picked up on a Queensland warrant. When they thought about it, they knew someone on parole in Victoria that went to Queensland and was only caught out when he was convicted of disqualified driving, where he was put on a community-based order. He was caught for his parole violation after the warrant bureau was reviewing outstanding warrants from Victoria. So, their advice was to get out of Queensland and stay out of trouble.

Katherine Pierce trusted their advice and told them, "I am considering nicking off within the next few days. I have nothing holding me in Queensland."

But she wondered out aloud, "How would I cope with Centrelink?"

In unison, the girls piped up and told Katherine, "You arrive where you are going and make an appointment with Centrelink and ask for assistance and advise on how to escape an abusive relationship."

The girls were on a roll. "Tell them the effect on the children from witnessing the abuse, that they have behavioural problems."

Which was not far from the truth. They encouraged her to go and were pleased when she agreed that it would be a good idea. Marcia had to tell Janet to back off a bit as Janet, in her enthusiasm, was going to help her pack her things that day but backed off when Marcia sensibly agreed with Katherine that within the next few days would give her more time to organise transport and decide what to take with them. They stayed another half hour to ensure Katherine at least had a plan and enough money to escape her misfortunes to make a better life anywhere else and out of the clutches of Stranger. Before they left, they had Katherine describe a coherent plan to them.

The girls were ecstatic that their plan had worked. Their main objective was to warn Katherine Pierce to keep her safe and out of harm's way. Janet was the more enthusiastic of the two, due to her nature and willingness to see the best in other people. Marcia was reluctantly enthusiastic and had doubts as to whether Katherine could maintain the plan. She knew Katherine was like Janet, in the way they agreed to ideas but were easily swayed by a better argument or an easier option.

Janet appeared her convivial self but spoke their thoughts out loud, "I wished we had warned Shelley."

Marcia was taken aback for a moment and reflected that they did warn her but she took no notice as she was enamoured by him at the time. They chided each other on being negative and the feelings of apprehension they both had as they drove away from her house. They agreed they had done all they could do and had her contact number to enable them to stay in touch if needed in the future. In other words, mission accomplished. They both knew that whatever advice is given, people make their own choices in the end. The easy or the hard road, most people would go for the easiest option and some people had more choices than others.

Chapter Fifty-Seven

Katherine Pierce was pleased that Janet and Marcia had visited and given her enough money to hire or buy a cheap vehicle to get out of Brisbane. This was the third time they had warned her about Stranger, even though they gave no specifics other than he was dangerous. She actually thought he was a pushover that would not harm her or her children. But she had to admit they had given her solid advice in the past. How to dodge urine tests, where to get a contraption to hold Adrianne's urine and keep the temperature hot enough to be valid. She laughed when Janet told her 'to do a poo when she was tested', that would certainly put the tester off as they'd leave the room and not watch the stream. She'd tried that once with the result Janet outlined. She'd jumped through the hoops her probation officer wanted her to do, which included drug and alcohol counselling and a psychological assessment. She'd stopped smoking pot and after clean drug tests, the drug and alcohol counsellor and probation officer stopped testing her. Janet had been right about that and gave her good counsel on how to get the psychologist on side. As Janet told her, 'all things or interventions cost money'. She liked the idea of doing a runner and starting a new life in Tasmania. She felt she could ask the girls for help if she was stuck, and they assured her they would help in any way they could to freeing herself from her current problems. When she thought about it, they were the only people she knew that she could rely on. Her own family had given up on her years ago or had she given up on them, she was not sure. Her mother was bi-polar and lived in Victoria, the father of her children had a new girlfriend and was currently in prison for breaching domestic violence orders. She knew she would have no difficulty explaining her situation and reasons for leaving Brisbane to Centrelink. She'd been in a domestic violent relationship with her previous partner and thought she knew the signs. She was haphazardly tidying up her house when the phone rang and disturbed her reverie of her future plans.

When she answered the phone, she recognised the caller as Stranger. His soft, dulcet tone made her forget the girls' warning that day. He asked her how she and the kids were going and apologised for not being in contact for over a month. He explained that he'd hurt his back at work and had a visitor from the United States and things were fairly hectic. He added that he'd love to catch up. She could not believe her own words. She said it was lovely to hear from him as well and agreed to see him at her place in two days' time as she had a lot to tell him. She had a lot to do. She packed bags for herself and the kids, all that they'd need to take, including their I-pads and the few toys they owned. Her kids were used to disruption and uncertainty and displayed a shyness and problematic behaviours of the insecurity in their young lives. Adrianne was the people pleaser, Tom the brat, behaved as the undisciplined child he was, due to being left unsupervised for hours at a time. Katherine claimed to love her kids, she did not spend quality time with them, which was probably a reflection of her own disruptive childhood. She and her family moved around a lot due to her unstable mother. She therefore felt that she had no ties to any particular place. She decided it was time to move on and was pondering whether to hire or buy a van. She would check out Gumtree, spend three thousand dollars on a van , and drive it until it ceased going. She would heed the girls' warning about driving unlicensed or disqualified. She knew she would have to show her driver's licence to hire a vehicle. She had failed to tell the girls she did not have a driver's licence. She decided to buy a cheap van and dump it if and when it broke down. Hopefully, it would get her to Tasmania. All she knew she needed to do was to get out of Queensland and start a new life somewhere else. The thought of new surroundings and adventure gave her the momentum to pack what was needed and to clean and tidy up all the excess belongings and rubbish, which were stuffed into the spare room. The furniture would have to stay.

Katherine had cleaned up her house ready for her departure and had been checking out vehicles to buy on Gumtree. She had her heart set on buying a Tarago van as it had enough seats for the children and enough space to enable her to pack what she needed to take. She was taken aback when Stranger pulled up outside her place in a Tarago van. He was alone.

He was surprised to see the house so neat and tidy. Katherine looked like she had made a major effort in cleaning up. She appeared glad to see him and he responded in a like way. After chatting about the weather and how things were going, Katherine admitted that her life at the moment was up to shit in regard to her Probation Order and the restrictions that were imposed on her. She knew he was also confined with the restrictions of a supervision order but had more freedom, with the exception of travelling interstate. She outlined her plan to escape and added she intended buying a Tarago van for three thousand dollars. Even though he had not planned in selling the van, as it wasn't his to sell, he offered her the van for three thousand dollars. She was ecstatic and immediately agreed to buy it then and there. She then told him of her plan to do a runner to Tasmania and intended on leaving within the next few weeks after buying a suitable vehicle. She was already packed and ready to go. Stranger could not believe his luck. She would leave her place willingly and he suggested she come with him as he had a place in the country where she could stay and organise her trip.

He'd dropped Holly at his house as he wanted to see Katherine Pierce alone to enable him to continue his manipulation of her as his next victim. He convinced her to leave for her new life today and gave her the easiest option to take. She believed in serendipity in that sometimes plans fall right into place. She believed that, if that occurred, it was the right thing to do. She was keen to get going after she checked out the van. It was perfect for the money, it had good seats, plenty of space to pack their belongings, and it was an automatic. She did not tell Stranger she did not have a driver's licence. She gave him two thousand dollars and asked if they could stop at the bank on the way. He could not believe his good fortune and offered to take her to Gatton via the bank. He watched her make the withdrawal, and even though she covered her pin number, he could tell by her action that the first two numbers were one and nine. *Not rocket science,* he thought to himself, *it is probably the year she was born.* It always surprised him how many people used this number, or the one either side. He reckoned he could work it out and knew that if you did not get it in three attempts, you'd lose the card to the machine. He knew he'd have to obtain her Centrelink number and was making plans in his head as he drove to the property on how to access her purse.

She seemed excited and happy and loved the little house on acreage he had taken her to. He explained that he would have to go to Brisbane for a few days as his overseas guest had gone to his house at Capalaba. As she unpacked the van, he decided to leave it with her and told her he would catch the train to Brisbane. She could drop him at the train station as he thought she would need the vehicle to do some food shopping. She was grateful for his thoughtfulness, and when she unpacked her meagre possessions, he rummaged through her purse. He had a didactic memory and only had to glimpse her Centrelink number to obtain it and file it in his memory. Stranger noticed she was a nervous driver, and as he left for Brisbane on the train, he hoped he had done the right thing by leaving the car in her not so capable hands. He was keen to see Holly to discuss their plans about Katherine Pierce and her kids. They had planned to kidnap her and had given themselves at least a month to enact their plan. Stranger felt a little uncertain about his seizing the opportunity therefore escalating the plan. He would need to obtain Holly's point of view.

He caught a taxi from the station and arrived home to find Holly searching for bugs or listening devices in his house. She had started checking the veranda when he arrived home and stopped doing what she was doing as he indicated he needed to talk. He told her what had occurred when he went to Katherine's house. Holly was impressed by his foresightedness to obtain her pin and Centrelink number but was not thrilled about selling the van as it was their alternative source of transport. Holly was insistent about either obtaining another form of transport or getting the Tarago van back. She explained that she did not know whether it was intuition or paranoia, but she felt very strongly about using Stranger's vehicle all the time. Stranger was starting to think she may be correct and now regretted his spur of the moment decision. The things they planned to take a few months fell into place within an hour. He now felt he had overreacted and thought it best to leave Katherine Pierce to her own devices for a few days.

Holly spoke his thoughts out loud, "I hope she stays at Gatton and not decide to do a runner."

Stranger wanted to phone her but did not make calls from his personal phone. He always used phone boxes, which were getting harder to find these days.

They also wondered whether to boost or borrow another vehicle that could not be traced. They looked at each other and laughed, they were so alike and simultaneously thought the same thought. *Hell, I've got Katherine's money, we'll do what she was going to do, buy something off Gumtree and never change the registration.*

Therefore, when it was dumped, it could not be traced to them.

Holly liked this idea, "That's what backpackers do, buy vehicles, drive them around, and either dump or re-sell."

She felt Gumtree was the best option as other car sales sites may be particular in checking the buyer. Gumtree, she knew from reports via Facebook, sold defective vehicles, the old buyer beware trick where no questions were asked or rather you could flash your driver's licence, anyone's licence really, to make a purchase. As long as you had cash to pay.

Holly was checking Gumtree and deciding what sort of vehicle to buy for three thousand dollars, Stranger was phoning the security firm Marcia had told him about. Before he'd get a system installed, he decided he would definitely check Marcia's system as he wanted to see her again. He could not get her off his mind and could not explain his feelings or attachment to her, other than she made him feel alive and he felt comfortable in her company.

Chapter Fifty-Eight

Denise had been checking the tracking devices on Stranger's vehicles religiously for the last few days. Both vehicles were stationary. However, on the fifth day, the Ford Territory moved, and Denise decided to let the tracking device do its work. She did not bother contacting Jed as it appeared to go to the shopping centre at Capalaba and had returned home. She sat there, wondering about their next move, when Jed called to say Stranger had called and arranged an appointment to have a security system installed.

He went to Stranger's house alone as Brian appeared to be incommunicado. Jed thought he knew what was going on and decided to check on him after he completed his phone call with Denise.

He told Denise, "I checked the premises two days ago under my own volition and removed the bug from the veranda as no one was home."

He felt that it was strange that both vehicles had not moved, he now thought they may have another vehicle. Denise told him the Ford had been on the move, was parked at Capalaba, and then went home. Jed decided to do a drive-by on his way to Brian's, he was not sure whether he would keep him on. He did not need an employee, even though he was a friend, to go missing in action and not answer his phone. Due to his suspicious nature, he decided before he got there that Brian was on a bender. He was famous for that. In the past, he had locked himself away for days at a time trying to drink himself to death. As he drove past Stranger's house, he noticed the Ford Territory was there as Denise had advised and Stranger was in the yard. He began to think of alternatives and the penny dropped, they may have other transport, or they might be catching public transport and or taxis.

He drove to Brian's and banged on his door and tried to look through the windows. One of his neighbours from the flat next door came out and asked him what did he think he was doing. Jed had to explain that he was worried about and looking for his friend, Brian.

"Okay, mate," said the neighbour. "He obviously is not home."

Jed still was not sure as his car was parked out the front. He pointed this fact out to him and thought, *what an arsehole*.

The neighbour laughed and said, "What are you, his keeper?"

And then he advised Jed that a car had come around and picked him up a few hours ago. As he drove off, he thought the guy was a nosey parker but then at least the neighbours kept an eye out for each other. That's something you take for granted when you live with someone. On the other hand, if you lived alone, who would know whether you were alive and well. At least he was alive and hopefully well. He tried his mobile again, it went straight to message bank. He was getting pissed off and decided to call in at Marcia's to give her the heads up about the call from Stranger. As he was driving there, he got a call from Denise who advised 'the target is on the move'. She gave him the GPS location and as he typed it in, he realised Stranger was coming his way, he'd have to divert, he took the next left and pulled over.

Stranger pulled up outside Marcia's house and rang the front doorbell. Marcia knew he would be coming to check out her new security system. She was with Brian, and they were about to have lunch on the back patio. When she answered the door, Stranger thought she looked annoyed and quickly realised he'd got that right. He told her he wanted to check out her security system. She showed it to him quickly and added that she had a visitor for lunch. She thought to herself, *of all the feeble excuses to drop in unannounced*. He felt and looked embarrassed and apologised for his lack of foresight and told her he had phoned the security firm she recommended and wanted to check out her system before committing himself. He noticed her attitude changed immediately, she appeared all red-faced and apologetic. She could not believe her own words, she actually apologised for being so abrupt and rude but added it was inconvenient to show him the system as she had a guest and they were just about to have lunch.

He took the hint and left, telling her, "I'll phone you and let you know when I want to come around in the future." As he drove away, he thought to himself, *that's why I like her, she has the guts to say no and enough manners to look embarrassed.*

Chapter Fifty-Nine

Brian and Marcia were halfway through lunch when there was a knock on the door. Marcia was beginning to like her new system, as she looked at the video screen and saw Jed standing on her front porch looking directly into the camera. As she answered the door, Brian came up behind her and greeted Jed amicably enough until he saw the look on his face. He appeared upset, even furious. Brian had a fair inkling as to why he might be furious, he knew he had fucked up and had gone missing for a few days and knew in his heart of hearts that he had done the wrong thing. He had not told Marcia about his slip up or lapse and had lied by omission to her. To Jed, he just lied outright, claiming his phone must be broken as he had received no calls or any missed calls from him. He could tell by the blank look on Jed's face that he did not believe a word he said.

Jed accepted a coffee and was all business after Marcia had told him of Stranger's visit that morning wanting to check out her security system. She said she'd got rid of him due to having Brian there and claimed he would be back later as he wanted to see her system before having Jed's company install one for him. Jed was pleased as he had wondered why Stranger was in the area and was doubly pleased that Marcia had curtailed him with a feasible excuse. Jed offered to drive Brian home, citing that he needed Brian for the job at Stranger's as he did not want Don involved in surveillance of him as it was on a need-to-know basis and the fewer people involved made it safer and less complicated. They did not need any leaks.

After they left Marcia's, Janet arrived. The last two weeks had flown by, and her kids were coming home in a few days. She had been in contact with Katherine, who advised her that she was on the run and had picked up a Tarago van and felt she was safe. She did not say where she was but assured Janet that she and her kids were fine. She offered to stay in touch and let her know when they arrived in Tasmania. They were both happy that she was out of Stranger's reach for the time being. Janet had not heard from Stranger or Holly during the last week and wondered out loud what they were doing.

She added, "I have a few more days of freedom and wouldn't mind going out for one more spree before my activities are curtailed by the return of my kids."

The kids were having a good time by all accounts. She'd phoned them every few days, they sounded happy and excited and described their adventures and outings they'd had with their grandmother.

Marcia wondered out loud whether she would have them for a bit longer, but Janet added, "I don't want to push the boundaries with my mother."

She knew from past experience that while her mother enjoyed the boys for a few weeks, she was getting old and now found them tiring and enjoyed sending them back home.

Janet was keen to have one more blast before she returned to her usual routine and the responsibility of children. They were having a bourbon and scheming about their next escapade when the phone rang. It was Stranger wanting to come around again to check the system. Marcia asked him to bring Holly around as well as Janet was there and wanted to arrange another outing before her kids returned home. He sounded pleased and agreed to bring her as Holly was getting a bit tetchy with the routine at home and claimed she was bored.

Marcia had to remind Janet not to get too excited or verbose about the security system as she was meant to have had it installed a year ago, not last week. She had to tell her to keep her own counsel or, in other words, 'shut your mouth' as far as it went. They arrived an hour later. Holly was pleased to see Janet and was led into the kitchen where Janet fixed her a drink. Stranger was pleased to have Marcia's undivided attention as she showed him the security lights, video equipment, and camera. He was impressed by the system and clearness of the image.

She added, "I don't keep any copies from the surveillance camera as I have no need to."

She further claimed, "Since installing it, I've had no prowlers."

As they chatted amicably about the deterrence factor of the system, Stranger reckoned he'd have one installed at his house.

When they entered the kitchen, Janet and Holly were scheming about their next adventure or escapade they would go on. They began to haggle about the best location, when, and where. They argued the for and against between the Gold Coast and Brisbane, Janet was determined to get her own way and have a change of venue. She argued convincingly that the Gold Coast was over-policed, and Brisbane was just plain boring after you'd been there once. Holly liked the Gold Coast but had to admit they had been lucky not to be caught in the police raid at the nightclub. She could not offer any opinion on Brisbane's night life as she'd never been there. Stranger and Marcia appeared to be laughing at them as they drank coffee. Stranger thought to himself, *the only places I know in Brisbane are either dives or where you picked up whores in Fortitude Valley*. He kept his thoughts to himself.

Marcia mentioned the Sunshine Coast as a destination that had good quality accommodation, night clubs, and restaurants that were within walking distance from each other. After checking different locations on the internet, they decided to go to Noosa Heads as it appeared to have all they needed for a good night or two out on the town. Even though it meant they'd have to go on a Sunday or Monday, due to Janet's children's return, this did not seem to worry Holly or Janet who were both after a good time. Janet and Holly were that keen to go, they left together after they arranged to visit Dianne at Capalaba to pick up supplies of coke and a few ecstasy tablets to ensure a good time. They decided against obtaining any hydroponic dope due to the fact it was hard to conceal and take due to the smell when smoked. They felt this was the careful option as they knew they would be in unknown territory therefore were not sure of the lay of the land. Even though she did not intend to, Janet left Marcia alone with Stranger.

Stranger, on the other hand, was glad he was alone with Marcia for the first time.

Chapter Sixty

Upon arriving home, Stranger reflected on the time he had spent in Marcia's company. He was impressed with the simplicity of her security system, it appeared to be a personal record of events rather than a linked system to a security firm. He liked the fact that she thought like him. She was one that took care of her own troubles and hell would freeze over before she contacted the police about any intrusion. She insisted it made her feel safe and deleted the recordings rather than tape over. A clean slate, she called it. He felt comfortable in her company. Whilst Janet and Holly were absent, she indicated she was not sure of the next excursion to the Sunshine Coast. He agreed with her, he liked more notice to plan an event. They had agreed in the end that spontaneous events were more exciting due to the unpredictable situations that could arise. By the time the girls got back from Dianne's they had decided what the hell, they'd go with the flow. They both felt uncomfortable about the lack of planning due to their love of stability, but the girls were so jazzed up when they got back, there was no stopping them now. He liked the way she laughed, he had a bit of a giggle at the girl's antics and felt he was on the same page as Marcy.

He was trying to sit in quiet contemplation, thinking of things he needed to do around his house and about the Gatton predicament as Holly had another line of speed and announced she was ready to go. They'd booked the accommodation while at Marcia's as they had to be there that night. He packed his two best outfits and some casual wear. He was ready in minutes and hoped Holly had packed all she needed as he had no intention of returning home due to her forgetfulness. He was keen to get there early to enable him to spend more time with Marcia. He knew Janet and Holly would distract each other enough to give him more time with her.

As they drove into the car park of the motel, he noticed Marcia's car was already there. This pleased him immensely. Was she as keen as he was, or had she been ambushed by Janet's enthusiasm as he had been by Holly's? As he signed in he could hear Janet's voice in the distance, she was trying to attract Holly's attention. They could get adjoining rooms if they wanted. Stranger could not believe his ears or luck, adjoining rooms, of course they'd like that option. He paid for two nights and was glad he'd taken his best outfit with him. He was going to turn it on tonight, he was out to impress her, he felt a need to manipulate her and have her under his control. He also knew this would not be easy as she was mindful and had an intelligence that was hard to define as he felt most women were easy to con and were stupid.

They had dinner at a nice restaurant on the boulevard that overlooked the beach. Stranger played the perfect gentleman all evening and even picked up the bill. Marcia was making comparisons between him and Brian. At first, she thought she definitely felt more comfortable with Brian due to his ability to keep a conversation going and his soft brown eyes. However, by her third drink, she began to see Stranger in a different light. He'd had a couple of bourbons and became quite lucid and relaxed as the night went on. While Brian dressed nicely, he was a bit flabby around the middle. On the other hand, Stranger looked physically fit and took a lot of care with his appearance. He had a good eye for detail as far as his clothing and personal touches went. In sum,

Brian was and could be a bit of a slob, Stranger was neat, well presented, and took great care in his appearance. But his blue eyes were strange and whilst he pretended to listen attentively to show he cared, she noticed that if she disagreed with him, a steely look would snap instantaneously in his eyes and that tended to move the argument in Brian's favour. The only set back with Brian was that he was unable to drink alcohol and Marcia decided she liked a drink or two. She decided to make tonight a good night. During dinner, she'd indicated to Stranger that she may turn in early as she did not feel like raging and going to a nightclub with the girls. By her third bourbon, however, she now felt she'd got her second wind and wanted to go back to the room before attacking the nightclubs. She'd not had a line of speed with Janet and Holly earlier and felt like one now.

They returned to the adjoining rooms before going clubbing. It had been decided that Stranger's room would be the drug-taking room and the girl's room, which was a bit larger, was for drinking alcohol. Janet and Holly had bought two grams of speed from Dianne as that was all they could get at the time. They were disappointed at first but after sampling the goods, they decided it was a good move, nothing like a good line of speed. Marcia and even Stranger had a couple of lines before leaving for the nightclub at eleven p.m.

They were allowed in and were surprised to see the place crowded on a Sunday. It was, however, nothing like the nightclubs on the Gold Coast. The clientele was much older and the music more their style. They had plenty to drink and the speed improved their dancing skills. They took to the dance floor like ducks to water. The music was from their era and Marcia, Stranger, Janet, and Holly danced together and had a lot of fun.

Stranger could not remember the last time or anytime he'd

had so much fun. It was the first time in years that he had gone anywhere without a plan. He liked the fact that he could handle his alcohol use in her company and genuinely felt an attachment or synchronicity. They went clubbing again on Monday night. Stranger could not believe he had two nights out in a row that he thoroughly enjoyed. He felt lucky as he looked at his attractive company.

Chapter Sixty-One

Hargreaves and Plummer was a hive of activity by the time Marcia and Janet arrived the following Tuesday morning. The tracking device had activated on Sunday and Brian and Jed had followed Stranger to the Sunshine Coast. They spotted Stranger, his daughter, and the girls hitting the dance floor at a local nightclub. They mingled in with the crowd and left without being seen. Brian had mixed feelings when he saw Marcia dancing provocatively with Stranger. He first felt anger, then jealousy, and then was fascinated by her sharp dance moves. What pissed him off the most was that she appeared to be having a good time with Stranger. He knew he had no right to be jealous but could not overcome his feelings of remorse as he watched them drink their bourbons and return to the dance floor between drinks. The more they drank, the more fun they appeared to be having. He wondered what she'd thought of his confession to his alcoholism and reflected back on their date and the chaste kiss at her front door. He still felt guilty in Jed's company as he had lied about the bender he had been on during the last week. He felt the lack of control over his drinking would be a turn-off for Marcia. *God, she must think I was and am a boring old fart*. He was startled as she entered the conference room, she looked alive and stunning.

Denise had called an extraordinary meeting, and everyone attended, including Margo and Kathryn. Margo updated them on Katherine Pierce's movements and advised she had not reported to her probation officer for a few weeks. She was on a final warning and an arrest warrant would be issued if she missed her next appointment. Marcia and Janet kept their knowledge about Katherine Pierce to themselves. Marcia did not want to let them know that they had been to see her and knew she intended on doing a runner, Janet was too hung over to care. They both knew that if they let the cat out of the bag, Denise and Carol would know they had been meddling when they had been specifically told not to.

Jed and Brian gave their report on their surveillance of Stranger and his daughter. Marcia indicated that they had not had time to advise them of the trip as it was a spontaneous decision. Her account of the trip did not shed too much light on Stranger's motivations or plans other than it was a social gathering. Marcia did not say anything about the drug use and Janet went along with it so as not to incriminate the pair of them. Janet looked at Marcia with admiration as she was a consummate liar by lying by omission.

Marcia did add that Stranger was very interested in having a surveillance set up at his house by Jed's firm. She gave the meeting the scenario of Saturday afternoon after Jed and Brian had left. Stranger had arrived later to check her security system.

As the meeting wound up, Jed had a call from Stranger and arranged a meeting for the next day to discuss his requirements and of course, give him a quote. Jed was delighted and Denise and Carol felt they would now be able to make some progress . ss. Janet and Marcia, on the other hand, felt uncomfortable with their betrayal of Stranger and Holly. They had to remind themselves of their goal of seeking justice for Shelley but had begun to have doubts. They decided the next meeting would be if there was any further information and details gleaned from the system.

After everyone had left, Carol was discussing Katherine Pierce's failing to report and the process of waiting for a fail to attend on a final warning. She could very easily slip away from their grasp as the warrant would be a return to court warrant rather than a return to prison warrant. If she left the State of Queensland, she could be on the lam for years and they would have no hold on her or Stranger. They decided they'd conduct a home visit that day to see if she had indeed done a runner. They felt that everyone else was having a bit of fun and excitement and felt the rush of anticipation of the unknown. Being natural born sticky beaks, they closed the office earlier than usual and went to her Morningside address. Within an hour, they thought they knew the answer. By all appearances, the house looked uninhabited, even though she had left her worldly possessions behind. They were reluctant to break in and made all their observations by peering through windows. Old habits die hard, and Carol waded through a bunch of weeds to discover one of the bedroom windows was slightly open. She was inside before Denise could protest, and after she let her in the front door, they searched the premises. Katherine Pierce and her kids weren't there, they had no idea where they were, and hoped they had done a bunk.

Marcia and Janet arrived at Janet's house after leaving the meeting feeling despondent after firstly lying by omission to the crew at Hargreaves and Plummer and, secondly, realising they knew Katherine had done a runner. They had encouraged her and aided her escape by giving her the funds to go. They felt like liars and fraudsters, which they knew they were, but they could not help feeling bad about the lack of trust they had in Carol and Denise at the time. As they drank coffee, they both knew that the mood they were in was probably due to their substance use over the last few days. Moreover, they were feeling sad about lying to

Carol and Denise. They felt like children again and mischievous ones at that. They liked being part of the team and decided on a course of action. Janet would phone Katherine and try to obtain her whereabouts and they would both come clean and tell the truth about their visit. They felt it would be easier to tell Carol rather than Denise. They knew Carol would understand them better as she'd known them for over ten years. They liked Denise, but they could not get over the fact that she was a copper, even a retired copper, she was still a copper. Whilst they trusted her, they were not sure of her response or attitude toward them. They'd have to tell the whole truth about helping Katherine Pierce and their use of speed in the company of Stranger and Holly. Their excuse for not saying anything at the meeting would be that they did not want to disclose this information to all those present.

Janet phoned Katherine and was surprised when she answered her phone immediately as she usually screened all calls. She sounded upbeat and happy. She had an energy in her voice that Janet rarely noticed before as she usually spoke in a monotone voice. One of disinterest of one that does not care anymore.

Janet asked her, "Where are you at the moment?" and told her, "The Probation Office thinks you may have done a runner."

They both knew the process and Janet need not explain that, once she missed her next appointment, a warrant would be issued. Katherine was reluctant to give her location to Janet at first.

Janet told her, "As long as you are not in Queensland, you will be all right."

Katherine went quiet for a minute.

The next thing she said was, "Me and the kids are at a friend's property in Gatton."

Janet told her, "You better get out of Queensland in the next few days as the warrant will only be good for Queensland and you need to get interstate pronto."

Katherine promised she would do this but needed to get her next benefit to fund the trip.

She told Janet, "I have bought a Tarago van from my friend, Peter."

And she thanked her and Marcia for the money to buy the van.

Katherine Pierce was very excited about the trip and starting a new life somewhere else. She told Janet that she had not decided on where to relocate and wanted to check out Victoria, South Australia, and Tasmania. God, she hadn't been outside Queensland since she moved there with her ex- partner and was both terrified and excited about the unknown. She blathered on about leaving her house at Morningside on the spur of the moment after Peter had sold her a van.

She told Janet, "I have only taken the bare necessities and have left all my furniture and white goods behind."

She now thought this was a silly thing to do as she would need these things if she was to set up house again anywhere else. As an afterthought, she asked Janet if she would put her stuff in storage. Janet had Katherine on speaker phone and Marcia gave her a nod to indicate they would put her possessions in storage. She slipped her a note asking, 'who is Peter'.

Katherine laughed and told her, "You know who Peter is."

And left it at that. She thanked Janet for the call and the help she and Marcia had given her and promised to stay in touch. As Janet hung up the phone, she shook her head and looked at Marcia and mouthed the name Stranger.

Crikey, they thought, they'd better get on their bikes, so to speak. Marcia phoned Hargreaves and Plummer and got the message bank that they were closed for the day. She left a message to contact her, stating it was urgent. For once in their lives, they were uncertain about what to do. What a day to close early. Marcia decided to phone Brian and Jed, both calls went unanswered. They'd try again later. Marcia thought about calling Peter Stranger but decided not to at this time. The feelings of amity towards Stranger, she now realised, was a drug induced fantasy and longing for male companionship. She now felt fear and loathing and realised she had nearly made a huge mistake in judgement and a goose of herself. She longed for the sensible Brian but was unable to contact him. She felt let down and possessive and wondered what he was up to at this moment. She'd had her chance at the meeting that day but was confused with Stranger's amorous attention, she was not rude to Brian, but she was certainly standoffish. She felt disappointed in her lack of judgement and told Janet how she was feeling. Her mate, Janet, fully understood her dilemma and confided in her that was part of his charm and dangerousness.

Marcia left to go home, and they decided to contact the team first thing tomorrow morning. They decided they needed an early night after dancing until they dropped. They both felt strung out, tired, and both had sore muscles from the previous night's gyrations.

Chapter Sixty-Two

Stranger was up early the following day. He wanted Holly out of the house when the security firm arrived at nine a.m. Instead of driving her to the train station, he ordered a taxi so she could catch the train to Gatton. He wanted her to befriend Katherine Pierce and her kids. A plan was forming in his head in regard to Katherine's demise and the possibility of Holly taking her identity and benefit to finance their escape. He knew from past experience that they would have to relocate and move around and knew that if they could continue receiving Katherine's Centrelink benefit it would assist them financially. First, he would have to ascertain whether Holly would cope with two children while pretending to be their mother, Katherine. He did not tell Holly of his plans, he wanted her to meet Katherine on her own terms, befriend the children at the same time, and see if she could comply with his plans. The only thing he told her was to make friends with her and her kids and find out as much as possible about their antecedents. As she got into the taxi he told her he would come out to Gatton later that day.

He was at home when Jed and Brian arrived to give him a quote. He noticed the short, muscled guy appeared to be the boss and did all the talking. The other guy appeared to be the gopher. They introduced themselves and Jed listened to what the client wanted in a security system and offered objective advice to enhance the client's needs. Stranger had to admit he was impressed with their approach to business and the price they quoted. He wanted the job completed as soon as possible. Jed indicated that they could start today as they had all the equipment required in their van.

He told him they would install a standard set up of video camera and security light sensor that would be hard wired. And due to him not requiring a response from a security firm if an intruder was picked up on the equipment, he would be able to install it today if he wanted it done so quickly.

Stranger let them inside and left them to do the work, saying, "I'll be back in a few hours."

Jed told him, "I'll wait for you to return and will give you the run down on what the system is be able to do."

As he left, Jed phoned Denise to tell her Stranger was on the move and they were unable to follow as they had secured the job and had work to complete.

Denise told him, "Don't worry about that as me and Carol will follow him in the camper van."

Stranger drove straight past Hargreaves and Plummer with Denise and Carol in hot pursuit. They did not have to keep up as the tracker gave a signal to their laptop. He headed out of town towards the semi-rural area in Gatton. It had taken over an hour to get to his destination. He drove down the driveway of a property that had a fibro house and a few sheds that were set back off the road. They noted the address and got out of the van for a closer look. He went inside carrying a few bags of groceries. No one came out to greet him and he left after staying ten minutes. By the time he got back to his truck, Carol had already driven further down the road before turning around to head back to Brisbane. They knew they could check the ownership of the property and would contact the land titles office on their return to the office. As they drove back, they wondered what this trip was about and who was at the property.

As they headed back to Brisbane, Carol stopped in front of the property and told Denise to knock on the door to see who was in there. Carol told her to ask for Joanne and to just say you're an old friend. Carol told her that she'd done this lots of times when looking for crims who had done a runner. Denise laughed as she got out of the van and walked down the driveway. The door was answered as she was about to knock. Denise was taken aback but continued with her ruse as Holly answered the door. Denise asked for Joanne and Holly rudely stated that no one by that name lived there and slammed the door. Denise knew she was looking at Stranger's daughter and thought she saw kids toys on the floor.

When she got back to the van, she muttered, "Hells Bells answered the door and there appeared to be children there as well due to toys I saw."

"God, Carol, how did you get away with that in the past?"

Carol told her, "I have a knack for making a nuisance of myself and have never had a door slammed in my face."

Carol decided to park the van and went down the road to see if anyone came out of the house. She'd made herself a cup of tea and settled in to observe. Denise thought it was a real hoot as she hadn't been on surveillance with Carol before and could not remember doing anything so absurd as a police officer. They were sipping their tea as Holly and two kids came out of the house and left in a Tarago van, which had been parked around the back of the house. Denise took the registration details as they followed them to the shops. Carol thought the kids looked familiar and told Denise.

They returned to Capalaba. They had some work to do or rather some checking to do. As they made a few calls, Carol was racking her brain about who the kids were. She knew she would remember as she had a legendary reputation for recognising faces.

Chapter Sixty-Three

Hargreaves and Plummer opened the next day earlier than usual. Denise and Carol were feeling jazzed up on their return from Gatton and were energised by their constructive use of time. They were acting like a pair of bloodhounds on a scent and began collating information they had gathered on the white board. The atmosphere in the office was like a contagion, affecting both Rosslyn and Richmond. The ownership of the van was the first piece of the puzzle that was listed on the white board. It was registered to a second-hand car dealer on the Golden Mile. Denise couldn't believe it when the registered owner appeared to be dodgy Roger Miller, who was well known to police for selling dodgy vehicles whose ownership could be hard to identify as he failed to transfer the ownership as required.

The property ownership appeared to be in a company name and had changed hands several times in the last fifteen years. However, one of the previous owners was named Stranger, who appeared to own the place in the late nineteen eighties. Could this be a link or a coincidence and seeing as Denise and Carol did not believe in coincidences, they were certain there was a link to Stranger. As they were discussing the possibilities, Marcia and Janet arrived.

Rosslyn had checked the previous night's messages and had told them that Marcia had left an urgent message on the answering machine.

As they settled into the conference room, Marcia disclosed

their conversation with Katherine Pierce the previous day. She had told them she had bought a Tarago van from Peter and was staying at his place in Gatton. They claimed they intuitively deduced that Peter was indeed Stranger. Carol and Denise could not fault their reasoning and were excited about this extra piece of information. Without incriminating themselves, Marcia and Janet told them that Katherine Pierce was going to do a runner as she had asked them to put her worldly possessions in storage. With this disclosure, Denise and Carol realised who the children were at the house and felt an urgency for action. They knew it would be out of the realms of their authority. They'd have to pass their information to the police but had to wait for a warrant to be issued. At the moment, it could only be passed on as intel rather than a welfare check into someone's safety. They would need further information to proceed with a welfare check.

As they were discussing which way to proceed, Jed and Brian arrived to confirm that they had completed the set-up at Stranger's house. They immediately switched on the remote access that activated cameras on his veranda, lounge-room, and kitchen, which were screened to Hargreaves and Plummer as Jed did not want to jeopardise his own security operation. Jed advised everyone that he had removed the illegal bugs he had previously installed. They were enthralled by what they were seeing live. Stranger was alone and preparing to go out. They now felt they had all bases covered and were not sure how to progress in regards to Katherine Pierce's safety. Marcia and Janet knew the promptest way to respond would be to phone Crime-Stoppers anonymously and mention guns or paedophilia. Carol and Denise knew that if they called in that old chestnut and nothing was located at Gatton, all would be lost in regard to their credibility in future operations. They decided to wait, watch, and follow. In the interim, they had leads to follow up, who owned the Tarago van and the property at Gatton.

Chapter Sixty-Four

The girls left the meeting feeling frustrated by the lack of action. They knew that one phone call to Crime Stoppers would throw the cat amongst the pigeons. All you had to mention was drugs, guns, and the endangerment of children and call in anonymously. They knew by experience how effective this trifecta was as they'd both been dobbed into authorities in the past. They both knew the nature of the dobbers, who were usually immature, jealous, and vengeful individuals who liked throwing shit into other people's camps. They thought it was totally un-Australian but knew statistically that 'we have become a nation of whingers and dobbers that are encouraged to do so by the government'.

Janet had one more day of freedom without her kids and was keen for action. Marcia, on the other hand, could see the wisdom in waiting for the right time but felt conflicted between their inability to help Shelley and their ability to throw some shit in Stranger's camp that would hopefully keep Katherine Pierce and her kids safe. They decided to call Katherine.

She answered straight away and sounded happy and relaxed and told Janet that she'd be leaving for her trip the next day. Janet was taken aback and was not sure what to say but gathered her thoughts quickly and told her she would put her stuff in storage and would keep in touch. Katherine thanked them again profusely and said a cheerful 'hello, goodbye' as she knew they would be together. The phone call settled their dilemma, they'd wait and let Hargreaves and Plummer do their thing.

Marcia decided to inform Denise of the call to Katherine Pierce and let her decide what to do. She'd feel better, like she'd done something constructive. They decided to go to the pub for lunch. They reminisced about the past fortnight's activities and the friendships they were developing with the straight crew at Hargreaves and Plummer. Over lunch, Marcia confessed to Janet how she had the hots for Brian and was confused as he totally ignored her at the meeting, was all business, and was not very friendly. She liked him better when he hung on every word and hung around like a love-struck puppy. Janet listened patiently and wanted her friend to be happy.

She had this thought as she sighted Brian entering the bottle shop at the pub. Janet gave Marcia a nod and a wink, drawing her attention towards Brian who had his rather large hands around the neck of a bottle of vodka. Marcia thought to herself that this is interesting and watched fascinated as he looked at several brands and read the labels. She had to laugh, really, vodka was vodka, and it didn't matter what brand it was, it was flavourless and had the same outcome. He looked up and caught a glimpse of someone watching him in his peripheral vision. *Oh fuck, it's Marcia.* He caught the look on her face and promptly returned the bottle of Absolute Vodka to the shelf. He knew he'd been standoffish at the meeting as he was still upset from his observations of her and Stranger on the dance floor. She gave him a wink and a nod, beckoning him over to the booth she was in with her friend, Janet. He came when he was called, and as he approached the table, Marcia thought of his lap-dog brown eyes that looked at her face. She felt herself lost in time and was genuinely pleased to see him. As he sat down, he began to make excuses in regard to buying the vodka for a friend but was not sure what brand they liked. Marcia thought, *sure, whatever pulls your chain,* and did not believe a word. She knew he was shopping for himself and had been tempted to break his sobriety. After he sat down beside her, Janet discreetly left the booth to play the pokies.

Marcia found herself making her own excuses for her behaviour with Stranger at the Sunshine Coast. Even though she had not seen them at the time, she now knew why he was standoffish at the meeting. She told him about their activities about warning Katherine Pierce and that they had told Denise, who advised a watch and wait surveillance. She admitted to feeling apprehensive about this situation. When it was time to leave, she discovered that she had been left in the lurch by Janet, who had left her at the pub with no transport. Brian drove her home where she invited him inside and literally pounced on him. She kissed him so passionately that he felt he was having an out of the body experience. He had never been seduced in such a fashion, he was in the hands of an expert who knew how to arouse, and he capitulated and felt totally sated. They laughed, talked, and giggled their way through the afternoon. He felt deliriously happy for the first time in years. No one had ever made him feel so loved and wanted. As he was about to leave, she jokingly told him to fess up about the vodka. He confessed everything to her, to his bender, and the fact the vodka was for him.

She grabbed him by the balls and said, "That wasn't too hard, was it?"

And they fell down laughing. After he left, Marcia had a long bath and was pleased that he had been truthful about the vodka. She felt that she could believe him and therefore trust him with her heart. She was humming Fleetwood Mac's 'You make loving fun' when the phone rang.

Chapter Sixty-Five

Stranger was alone at home feeling at a loose end. He'd started getting used to having the company of Holly and began reminiscing of the time he had spent alone with Marcia at the Sunshine Coast. He knew he'd have to go to Gatton for a few days but before he left, he decided to phone Marcia to arrange to take her to dinner. He let the phone ring and expected an answering machine or voicemail, but it rang off the hook. He was pissed off that she was not at home to answer his call. He knew it was an unreasonable assumption as he had no ties to her. He was feeling like he did as he would probably not see her or be in her company again. He had left Holly with Katherine and her children for over a week and knew their plan for murder would be on the table when he returned. He was mindful of what Holly said in relation to using the same vehicle and had an old motor bike that he had always parked at the back of his house. He decided to take it to Gatton and leave his Ford Territory at home for the time being.

He rode the bike around the block a few times to ensure it still worked and to give him a bit of practice as he had not ridden it for a few years. He rode out of the city, carefully as he did not trust other drivers. Once he hit the open road, he felt rejuvenated and alive. By the time he arrived, he felt the excitement with a touch of apprehension before the kill. He knew this feeling well. Holly was glad to see him. She wanted to talk to her dad and co-conspirator alone. She explained that she had a reasonably good time with their targets, she indicated that Katherine was preparing to leave today to begin her new life. She was starting to panic.

She told her father, "I got Katherine stoned and pissed every night where we discussed our lives, experiences, and plans."

Holly had found out a lot about her without disclosing anything of much value about herself. She obtained her pin number for her bank account by running errands to the shops using her key card. It was two years after her birth year. When she ran the messages, she took the kids with her as Katherine was too hung over to come at the time. She'd done a lot of background activities to ensure their plan would succeed. She went to Centrelink with the kids and told them of her plan to move interstate due to domestic violence issues. She'd been coaching the kids during the last week to call her mum. Katherine was Mum One, she was Mum Two. She was a chameleon, a master imitator who not only talked and acted like Katherine, she changed the colour of her hair to looked like her, even though she was taller. During their drinking sessions, Holly discovered that Katherine Pierce had no contact with her family or the father of her children. She'd described her family as a bunch of losers with nothing to lose. Her kids had never met their grandmother and she, made no effort to see them in their short lives. Her ex-partner had a new girlfriend and was in prison. The only people she knew who had shown some interest in her life were a few criminals in Brisbane. Holly tried everything she knew to find out who these people were, but Katherine would not disclose their names. She'd told Holly not to bother trying to find out who they were as they were her only friends and she did not want to tell her.

Holly had thought about everything she could possibly do before they had their fun with Katherine. On one of her trips to the shops, she switched the number plates of the van with another Tarago van that was the same colour. She was not sure whether it would be noticed immediately by the other owner and discussed this concern with her father. Stranger was not sure either. How observant are some people? It may be noticed immediately, or it may take a few days to notice the change in plates. They were discussing this issue when young Tom came to the veranda where they were sitting, first claiming he was hungry then wanting to go to the toilet. Holly jumped up and attended to his second need first, then fixed him a bowl of fruit salad that she had made and placed in the fridge.

Stranger looked at his daughter with admiration at her parenting skills. She appeared to enjoy looking after the kids. Tom and Adrianne were enjoying their fruit salad and yoghurt. Holly was appalled by Katherine's parenting skills and the lack of care of her own children. She'd let them eat anything and had spent little quality time with them. Holly reckoned it took about three days of good food to notice a change in their behaviour. She'd been having fun playing games with them, listening to them, and feeding them proper food. She added spending a week with Katherine Pierce was an intolerable situation that drove her to distraction. She fed her kids lollies, cookies, and muesli bars, feeling that this was a healthy option. She used the television and their I-pads as a built- in babysitter. Holly claimed that was why they appeared to be little shits. She took the superior attitude one with no kids takes, if they were fed properly, listened to, and disciplined, they would be easier to manage. She appeared to be right about that at the moment and Stranger noticed a marked improvement in their behaviours. The kids liked Stranger as well as they had only happy memories and experiences with him when he took them for fun outings at the theme parks at the Gold Coast.

"Speaking of the mother from hell, where the hell was Katherine?"

Holly blinked, swallowed, and said, "She's trussed up like the pig she is and is in one of the containers at the back of the property."

She went on to explain the previous night's activities where they had consumed a fair amount of alcohol and pot. She claimed Katherine was fine one minute and then, all of a sudden, she turned into a maudlin bitch. One minute she was making plans to do a runner, then suddenly she became inert on the couch, claiming her life as it was sucked. She was on a depressive cycle and had the 'woe is me' diatribe going all night. Holly could not handle it and left her to her own devices and went to bed. A few hours later, she woke to the sounds of Katherine screaming. She had tripped over her own shoes as she scrambled to the door to find out what was happening. The kids were in bed asleep, and the screams were coming from the bathroom.

Katherine was on the floor screaming, "I am going blind."

She told Holly she thought she was putting eye drops in her sore eyes. Holly noticed the action lotion bottle on the floor and promptly started to wash her eyes with a saline solution. She gave her a drink laced with Rohypnol, which affected her quickly, she passed out. Holly carried her to the container and tied her up, hands and legs tied behind her like a trussed pig. Holly did not like her and was not sure what to do next. She decided to superglue her eyes shut to teach her a lesson. Then her father arrived.

After she told him what she'd done, she felt better. He'd take control of the situation as he'd done before when she'd slipped up at the Gold Coast.

Stranger sat in silence for a few minutes trying to figure out what to do next. This escalation of events was not in the plan. He went into see Katherine, who was lying on a mattress on the floor inside the dark room. She had started to come to her senses. He spoke to her in a soft voice, telling her that she'd be all right in a few hours. He loosened her ties and told her she could not see as she was in the dark to try to protect her eyesight and that the only thing they could do at this time was to keep calm and wait for daylight to come. He knew she would not see daylight. The last thing Katherine Pierce heard was the sound of her children screaming as she drifted into the next life.

Stranger packed her torn and ruined body into a tent bag and stuffed it into the back of the Tarago van. Holly and the kids were almost ready for their road trip by the time he returned to the house. They'd both been up all night. After they tortured, tormented, and had turns sexually assaulting her, they had the kids scream their little lungs out just for fun. Holly had been coaching the little buggers on their trips to town. They yelled and screamed for their mummy as Holly told them she was a long way off and they needed to be loud. At one stage, Stranger had to stop what he was doing to check out what was happening, they sounded like they were getting murdered. Katherine was still out of it and kept trying to open her eyes and her screams were reduced to sobs and groans. They both fucked her, using their imaginations, fingers, and fists, and Stranger became fascinated and extremely turned on when Holly's sexual capacities became apparent. She was a bloody mess when they had finished with her. Stranger had the last turn and strangled her as he climaxed.

They returned home to Capalaba where Stranger unloaded the tent into the boat and told Holly to leave with the kids. He told her he would catch up with her in about a week's time as he had plenty to do before he could join her. He added that if she did not hear from him during the next week, she would have to go it alone.

Chapter Sixty-Six

Denise was alerted to movement at Stranger's house when the surveillance camera reacted in the front yard. She'd been unable to sleep and had night terrors. She'd been awake since three a.m. and was unable to get back to sleep. She had a fear of foreboding. She could see the Tarago van pull up behind his vehicle and saw him unload what appeared to be camping equipment into the boat. The tent looked heavy as it took two people to lift it into the boat. The other person looked like Katherine Pierce. Denise wasn't sure but had the feeling that she was witnessing a crime in progress. She continued watching and saw the Tarago van leave, driven by a woman with two children on board. She'd have to get Rosslyn and Carol to look at the footage later as they both had a good eye for detail. That is Rosslyn for the subtlety of difference that others could not see, and Carol was a one-percenter who could recognise a face by looking at the eyes. Whether Denise was right or wrong, she knew she had to call the team in for action. Jed and Brian would be called to follow the boat, and Carol and Rosslyn could check the tape and would head for Gatton to where they thought and knew Katherine Pierce had been hiding out.

It appeared that everyone that worked for Hargreaves and Plummer were having a sleepless night as they immediately answered their phones. They all sounded alert and ready to move at a moment's notice. Brian was ready to go when Jed arrived to pick him up. They'd both been unable to sleep and, to their surprise, they'd both had nightmares of impending disasters that they were unable to stop. As a result, they'd been unable to return to sleep and had been pacing the floors of their respective properties. They were glad to be on active duty again and were energised by the adrenaline boost they got when they were called for active surveillance.

Stranger had just left his property and appeared to be heading for Carbrook. He was in no hurry, kept to the speed limit, and was careful not to draw any attention to himself or his driving. They followed him at a safe distance. He was heading for his previous launching site at the vacant block of land at Carbrook. On this assumption, Jed and Brian had the foresight to hitch Rosslyn's tinny to their vehicle before they left home and went to the Redland Bay boat ramp and entered the water downstream from where Stranger was about to launch. They would have enough time to catch up with him even though his boat was bigger and faster. They had the advantage. They had the tracking device on the boat and need not try to keep up with him. He was a creature of habit and after he left Carbrook, he headed towards the south end of Russell Island and on towards the Gold Coast. It was a beautiful day for boating, and at this early hour, there were a number of boats on the water. It was a picturesque scene. Jed began to daydream about fishing and Brian was having fanciful thoughts about his next date with Marcia. They pulled themselves together and came out of their reverie when they noticed Stranger's boat stop near the fishing huts on South Stradbroke Island. He jumped quickly out of the boat, unlocked the padlock, and entered the hut that Marcia had previously described. They watched as he manhandled a tent bag with great difficulty and carried it into the shack. Brian had anticipated that, in following Stranger, they'd need to have some evidence to present and had borrowed Marcia's camera. He took a few shots and looked at Jed. They both thought simultaneously, *tent bags that size aren't that heavy.* They heard a chainsaw start up. Something was not right. Jed wanted to go ashore to have a closer look but decided to phone in a report to Denise, who was co-ordinating the surveillance activities. She advised them to stay put for a while and then, as an afterthought, instructed Jed to get closer if he could do so without being seen. She added that she would contact the Gold Coast Police for assistance.

Rosslyn and Carol drove straight to the property at Gatton as they assumed the Tarago van would return there. They waited an hour before deciding to go inside to have a look around. Rosslyn was checking doors and windows of the house, Carol was looking for a front door key amongst the pot plants on the veranda. It did not take long to find the front door key, third pot on the left-hand side. They felt apprehensive as they entered the vacant house. They had both slept badly and had a premonition of an unhappy ending for Katherine Pierce. Carol understood this feeling well due to her past dealings with clients who unfortunately had met with a grizzly end due to circumstances they could not control. Some people were designed to have a sad end no matter how hard one tried to guide them to a better future. The place was empty, no one was there, and someone had tidied up. There was no use looking any further and they decided to return to the office to watch the surveillance tape as Denise was keen for them to have a look at the footage from Stranger's that was taken that morning.

Jed couldn't stand the suspense of wondering what Stranger was doing inside the hut and waiting for the police to arrive. He had to have a closer look. He decided to go ashore and swam from the boat, landing a few huts down from the one Stranger occupied. Brian drifted the tinny and parked in front of the hut. He was the cockatoo in that he'd alert Jed if needed. Jed was good at sneaking around and Brian did not see him until he was at the side of Stranger's hut. Just as soon as the chainsaw noise ceased, Brian's phone rang, he'd have to answer it, it was Marcia. Stranger came out of the hut looking agitated and dressed in a coverall suit that was covered in blood. Brian was momentarily distracted by the phone call and was almost a disaster as a cockatoo. He did, however, pull himself together as he noticed Jed who was in no-man's land and on a collision course with Stranger who was looking around the hut. . The only thing Brian could think to do was to hurl a bit of verbal abuse over the phone directed at Marcia pretending they had kids as he took a photo of their target. He shouted fuck off a few times as loud as he could for good measure. The commotion he caused alerted Jed, who did a quick about face and hid behind the hut, he had not been seen by Stranger. He had been unable to sight any activity in the room as it was wrapped in plastic sheeting, making it impossible to see what was inside the hut. Jed made his escape and Brian could see him by one of the huts that was nearby. Brian motioned him to stop and wait for the 'all clear' as Stranger was marching around his hut looking for something that he thought was there but found nothing. When given the 'all clear', Jed swam back to the boat and an excited Brian showed him the only photo he'd been able to take. To them, it looked like a crime in progress. As they pulled away, Jed phoned Denise but was unable to connect due to poor reception. They were in a black spot and would have to move. They headed towards Southport on the Gold Coast and phoned Denise from there.

Denise answered immediately and sounded frustrated. She'd not been able to convince any of her cohorts on the Gold Coast to act on the information she had given them. Jed explained the situation in a succinct manner and told her they had a photo of Stranger on the veranda. He appeared to be covered in blood. Denise asked or rather demanded he email it to her at once. Thank God for smart phones. He emailed the photo and hoped it had enough clarity to get the Gold Coast police on the move. They returned to Redland Bay and went immediately to Hargreaves and Plummer at Capalaba.

Chapter Sixty-Seven

Marcia hung up the phone, nobody tells her to fuck off and gets away with it. She'd have his guts for garters when she caught up with him. The phone had been on speaker phone and Janet just sat there with an amused look on her face. They'd both heard partial bits of the conversation as the reception broke up throughout the call. Marcia was fuming and spitting chips. Christ, she was cranky.

Janet, on the other hand. was thinking out aloud, "What was that all about? You don't have kids and he doesn't like fishing. There must be something going on."

After Marcia calmed down, Janet, for the first time in her life, was the voice of reason.

They both thought about their mission and Katherine's escape from her warrant, her safety, and decided to phone her mobile. The call went straight to message bank, they did not leave a message and hoped Katherine Pierce would recognise the number and phone back. They'd both been feeling skittish and worried about her and had been unable to sleep. Janet had arrived at seven a.m. and they had been discussing options. They felt the need for action and considered ways to upset the apple cart. They decided to meddle and throw some shit in Stranger's camp, so to speak. They decided to go for the trifecta, drugs, guns, and paedophilia, and phoned Crime-stoppers. Marcia made the call after she calmed down. She was taken seriously and reported concerns about her friend and children's safety and gave

Stranger's address at Gatton. They both felt gleeful after the call, not that they liked causing mischief, but again they felt the call may cause some momentum and action from the police.

Marcia called Brian and when he answered he sounded sheepish. He apologised for his response to her last call and told her things were starting to move with their surveillance of Stranger. He told her he and Jed were at the office at Capalaba discussing the case with Denise. The phone call ended abruptly, and this did not appease Marcia who had decided to go to the office to find out about the new developments. They were deciding on whether they should attend Hargreaves and Plummer, and what to say when they got there, when Janet's mobile phone rang. Marcia answered it and thought she recognised the voice at the other end. It was not Katherine. It was someone enquiring about a missed call from that number. It sounded like Holly trying to imitate an Australian accent. Marcia sounded snappy and said it must be a wrong number and hung up. She was not sure of what she thought as she had not spent a lot of time with Holly. She told Janet what she was thinking as the phone rang again, the call register listed the caller as Katherine Pierce. Marcia nodded to Janet and answered, trying to disguise her voice, and put the phone on loudspeaker so Janet could hear.

Janet listened carefully to the voice at the other end and gave Marcia the thumbs up as Marcia hung up again stating, "Wrong number and don't call back."

Now they thought they knew something had happened to Katherine Pierce and wondered why Holly had her mobile phone, which was most unusual. They decided to go to the office at Capalaba to enlighten the others of this new development.

Chapter Sixty-Eight

Stranger felt an uneasiness he rarely felt in the past. He'd always been careful and usually disposed of his victims under the cover of darkness. He now felt uncertain and exposed due to the escalation of their original plan and due to the propensity of the situation at Gatton. He cursed his daughter under his breath as he prepared the parcels and burly he had yet to dispose of on the other side of Stradbroke Island. He noted the difference between the cutting up and disposal of lonely boy compared with Katherine. He did not know or care for lonely boy and had the advantage of being chemically enhanced at the time. On the other hand, he knew Katherine Pierce and although he intended to kill her as she was the perfect victim, he looked at her lifeless body and almost felt sorry for her. This made the grizzly task of chopping her up more difficult than it should have been. He felt an urgency to complete the job and wondered about the guy in the tinny. He looked familiar, but he could not be certain as it may have been his heightened state of perplexity or his imagination. He threw a lot of bleach around the hut after he loaded the boat with burly and Katherine's remains. He felt the need to get out of there and thought he could return at a later date to clean up properly. He'd always been careful, not this careless. As he drove the boat past and through the gap between North and South Stradbroke Island, he headed towards his dumping area. He thought he saw a police boat heading towards the lee side of South Stradbroke. All he could do was dump the body and head to Gatton to ensure Holly got away safely.

He returned to Carbrook, where he had launched the boat. He did not bother hooking it up to his car but rather left it there. He'd phone Jack later to tell him where it was. He needed to move quickly and got into his car and headed out of Brisbane toward Gatton. As he was driving to Gatton, his phone rang, it was Holly. She told him that she was at a caravan park in the Tweed Valley but had left her purse and driver's licence at Gatton. She was staying at a park that did not need or take her registration or indeed her licence number. She told her father she had been busy removing any trace of Katherine at the property and therefore overlooked her own identifying paperwork at the house.

He told her, "I'm on my way there and will clear the place out and meet you at the caravan park."

The only other concern she felt was a phone call to Katherine's number that she had not answered but phoned the missed call back to discover that the person who answered denied making the call. She added this made her suspicious as she did not expect any calls to Katherine's phone number as they both thought she would not be missed.

Stranger told her to ditch the phone.

Chapter Sixty-Nine

Denise had been on the job early. She'd been tracking the vehicles Stranger had been using and had forwarded the photo of Stranger to the Gold Coast Police. They now seemed interested and were given directions and the location of the hut on South Stradbroke Island. All she could do was cross her fingers and hope for the best. She noted that the boat was on the move and moving away from the hut and across the bar between North and South Stradbroke Island. Then it returned to Carbrook where it remained in a stationary position. The Ford Territory was on the move, heading out of Brisbane. She'd been able to contact the police boat, alerting them to the fact that Stranger had left the hut. They in turn were unable to sight the boat and were heading toward the hut.

As she got off the phone, Jed and Brian had arrived. Denise felt an urgency to move and before they could debrief, she directed them to follow Stranger.

She told them, "Go straight to Gatton as he's left Carbrook and did not stop at his property but headed out of town."

She'd made this assumption from past experience. The timing would be crucial if they were going to catch him. By the time Marcia and Janet arrived, Brian and Jed had left on their chase. Within half an hour, the rest of the crew were there getting an update on the current circumstances. They were all there, with the exception of Brian and Jed who were heading toward the final destination. They were all paying attention and after Denise had shown the photo of what appeared to be a bloodstained Stranger, they all felt sick to the stomach. Marcia and Janet could not help their response as they blustered out all the details they knew, which included the phone call to Katherine's phone and the anonymous call to Crime-Stoppers.

Rosslyn, Carol, and Richmond immediately left the office in the campervan and headed towards Gatton. Denise stayed behind to direct the surveillance and police action as she was the only one with any hope of being taken seriously. Marcia and Janet stayed behind and were feeling helpless. Denise had to make a few calls to get the ball rolling and needed the girls at the office as she wanted them to contact Katherine Pierce's mobile. Before they did this, she wanted to clear her head from the diabolical situation that was developing. She could feel the adrenalin pumping through her body. . Denise could identify this type of excitement and knew she would have to calm down before making any further decisions. Brian and Jed both operated on adrenalin and could act impulsively at times. Marcia and Janet were beyond that feeling of excitement and continued feeling sick as they had convinced themselves of their failure to protect Katherine Pierce.

The Gold Coast Police phoned Denise after they'd checked the hut. It looked like a crime scene, and they had cordoned the. hut off and were waiting on the forensics team to arrive. To her disappointment, they had missed the boat that had left before they had arrived. Denise gave all the information she had about the boat's movements and co-ordinates on her GPS. She then gave the address at Gatton and advised them that her surveillance team and investigators were on their way there and would need back-up as Stranger was dangerous and sometimes unpredictable.

After she completed her calls, she made coffee for herself

and the girls. As they discussed what had occurred on Janet's phone, Denise decided it would be best if Janet called Katherine Pierce as she was the one with the contact details and she was the one who spent the most time with Holly and believed she had recognised her voice on the previous call. Denise now felt in control as she had pulled as many strings as possible and had called in favours from all her contacts to ensure an end to the case. Before she allowed Janet to make the call, she told them the call may have repercussions for their safety. She warned Janet that if the call was successful, she could be placing herself and family in grave danger. Marcia looked at Janet and gave her a nod. Some people gambled on games of chance, others, like them, gambled with life. They both lived life on the edge and the potential for disaster was imminent. They both laughed as they thought to themselves, *danger is my middle name*.

Janet phoned Katherine Pierce's mobile. It went straight to message bank.

She left a message, "Hi, Katherine, this is Autumn, where are you? Give me a call," and left her number.

Chapter Seventy

Stranger drove on regardless of the consequences of the morning's activities. He had the feeling that he was running out of time and knew he would have to relinquish his property at Gatton. He had to constantly remind himself not to speed on the motorway as being stopped by police was the last thing he needed at this time. He was deep in thought about what he needed to do when he got to his house at Gatton and had disturbing thoughts in regard to Holly's last phone call. Although Holly did not know who Autumn was, he did and he remembered that she was a mate of Katherine's. Not a good mate but one that would be concerned if she was unable to contact her as she was part of the criminal fraternity. He cussed under his breath. He had a lot to do. God knows where she left her purse, he'd have to check the house and find that before he retrieved the stash of money he had concealed behind the wall in of one of the bedrooms at the house. His parents had lived like paupers, and after their untimely demise, he discovered they had fifty thousand dollars in the bank. . Over the years, he had added to the account and now had roughly a hundred thousand dollars. It was his rainy-day money, and he now knew he would have to retrieve it if they were going to get away. He'd have to smash a hole in the wall as over the years he had dropped money down a hole in the top of the fibro wall.

Their plans were ruined, and he knew they would have to make a disconnect from the system. No Work Cover and no Centrelink benefits to rely on to fund their journey. They would have to become anonymous, and he wondered what they'd have to do with the children. For the first time in years, he was worried and distracted, he did not notice he was being followed. All he could think about was prioritising what needed to be done as he had no intention of being caught. On the other hand, he had no idea what they would do, or where they would go. All he knew was that he needed to get out of Queensland. He realised he would be leaving the only place he knew and felt connected to. He had never been anywhere else and only had friends through the criminal network he met in prison. He and Holly would be alone in a totally new environment and would have to reinvent themselves. He felt scared and could identify the nervous tummy of excitement and fear of the unknown. The only thing he knew was that he did have an escape plan, his last resort.

He did not notice the Hyundai Excel that was parked across the street as he pulled into the driveway at his house at Gatton. He was feeling out of sorts and so distracted that he could not think clearly. He retrieved the key from under the pot plant and entered the house. It was spotless. Holly had at least done a good job of cleaning up. He left his driving gloves on as he did not want to leave any fingerprints and hoped that Holly had thought of wiping all prints off the surfaces. Where the hell did she leave her purse? He was wasting precious time. He looked everywhere he thought someone would leave it. He made one last call to Holly as he searched, she could not remember.

He then told her to ditch Katherine's phone again. He looked everywhere, and after he searched all cupboards, chairs, and drawers, he was about to give up when he finally found her purse and papers on top of the fridge. Who would think to put it there? Then again, she probably put it there out of reach of the children... He then smashed a hole in the wall of the second bedroom, ironically the room where Katherine and her kids had stayed in when they were there. The money his parents had squirrelled away was where he had left it years ago, wrapped in plastic in a backpack, the miserable bastards. The bundles of money he had haphazardly chucked down the hole was harder to find. He could only find forty thousand dollars, and after smashing the entire wall in, he had lost one bundle of ten thousand dollars. He also retrieved the handgun he had bought years ago and spent the next twenty minutes cleaning it and loading it. Just in case he would have to use it in his escape. He was pissed off, after all ten grand was ten grand, but he knew he could not spend all day looking for it. He stuffed all he found into the backpack when he thought he heard a noise outside. Was it his nerves, paranoia, or was there someone outside? He quietened his mind and took some deep breaths and listened carefully. The psychological intervention his parole officer made him complete came in handy at times of great stress. He could hear nothing, and this made him feel more unsettled.

Jed and Brian were the first to arrive and had parked across the road from Stranger's house. They saw him arrive and waited and watched. Rosslyn, Carol had sighted his car on the motorway and had followed him to Gatton. He'd been in the house for an hour. Jed, in the meantime, was in communication with Denise who had told them to wait as the police were on their way. Jed walked over to the van to tell them to wait until the police arrived as per Denise's instructions. They all felt they were waiting too long but no one was prepared to piss Denise off at the time. They knew the time they had would be limited and half expected Stranger to get in his car and drive out in front of them. They were losing patience when two police cars arrived. A general duties car followed by an unmarked car. Jed took the leadership role and went to the unmarked car to explain the situation.

He told police, "We have been watching and waiting for over an hour and the target is still inside the house."

There were two entrances, a front and back door and his car was parked in the front yard.

The detectives from the child abuse unit took control and it was decided to take him by surprise rather than knock on the front door. They all took their positions; the police would take the main entrance, the crew from Hargreaves and Plummer would cover the back door. The shout went up.

"Police, open up," as they pounded the door in with a sledgehammer.

Stranger immediately sprang into action and took off through the back door, he ran towards the containers that were concealed in the backyard. Christ, he was right, there was someone outside. He should have trusted his first instinct as he was rarely wrong.

The police shouted, "Go. Go. Go."

And with that signal, Richmond took off after Stranger.

In the preceding chaos, the crew from Hargreaves and Plummer were closer to the containers than the police. As they all ran towards the containers, the traps that were set went off as they were triggered. Spring-loaded poles with barbwire attached and dog traps seemed to be going off everywhere. The only one who was making any ground on Stranger was Richmond.

Rosslyn screamed, "Bang, you're dead."

As Stranger turned and fired off a few rounds at the pursuers. Richmond fell to the ground and did not move. By this time, Rosslyn was hysterical as she charged toward the dog with no regard for her own safety. Richmond lay motionless on the ground. The police and crew from Hargreaves and Plummer were injured and trapped in vicious dog traps and no one was in a position to pursue him. All they heard was the sound of a motorbike heading off at high speed.

Epilogue

The phone rang at Hargreaves and Plummer. Denise answered on the third ring, it was Carol.

"Oh dear! Oh no! Oh fuck! Is he all right?"

Marcia and Janet looked at each other and thought the worst.

"What's happened?"

Denise explained the incident very succinctly. The crew and some police had been injured as they were trying to apprehend Stranger, who had got away. Everyone who was injured was either treated by paramedics at the scene or taken to hospital with serious injuries.

"Fortunately, no one from our crew has been hospitalised and the only one who wasn't injured was Richmond. I've told them to return to Capalaba after they have been patched up by the ambulance service."

Marcia asked about the extent of the injuries and was told by Denise, "I guess we'll see that when they arrive back at the office."

"Okay, girls," Denise was back in control, "Here's a hundred dollars, go and get a box of Jim's or Jack's and some snacks from the bottle shop at the Tavern."

The girls did what they were told and left quietly. They started to think that Denise is all right. They liked to be included.

As they were browsing at the bottle shop at the Tavern deciding what to buy, they saw Jack Donnelly in the spirit section and said hello. They decided to buy Jim Beam cans as that's what they liked to drink and spent the change on crisps and salted peanuts.

They mentioned to Jack, "We had a lovely time on your boat with Peter and we are wondering where he is as we have not heard from him for a few days."

Then they introduced themselves and told Jack, "He has our mobiles if he needs to contact us," and left it at that.

Jack said, "I'd like to talk to him as he has not returned my boat."

He agreed to pass the message on if they'd do likewise. They agreed to do this.

Janet and Marcia were on their second bourbon by the time the crew got back to the office. They all looked knackered and had bandages, band-aids, and betadine on the numerous scratches and welts that were all over their arms and bodies. Rosslyn had a huge welt across her face where she was whacked by a tied down branch as she ran towards Richmond. Richmond appeared very subdued.

Carol said, "If it wasn't so hideous, it would have been hilarious. I came running around the back and tripped on a paver. From where I was laying, I saw everyone go down like ten pins. Because we were out the back, we ran into the traps first. The police copped the worst of it, we copped the bamboo, they copped the bear or dog traps."

"Fucking hideous and the prick got away," Rosslyn added. "After Richmond did not move, I thought he was dead. Then I remembered I had to tell him to get up."

Jed and Brian stoically handled their injuries, they were battered and bruised and would live to fight another day.

Denise called the meeting to order after Margo and Kathryn

arrived. She told those gathered that Hargreaves and Plummer had completed their investigations and were handing all evidence obtained to the Queensland Police Service.

She said, "We now have some concrete evidence. We have a photo of Michelle Farmer getting into his car in Fortitude Valley, we have his Ford Territory and three crime scenes. I'd like to thank everyone involved with this investigation, especially Janet and Marcia who were very brave and courageous in obtaining crucial evidence in this matter."